The Schemers & Viga-Glum

TWO SAGAS OF ICELANDERS

THE SCHEMERS & VIGA-GLÚM

Bandamanna Saga & Víga-Glúms Saga

TRANSLATED BY
GEORGE JOHNSTON

The Porcupine's Quill

CANADIAN CATALOGUING IN PUBLICATION DATA

Main entry under title:

The schemers & Viga-Glúm : two sagas of Icelanders

Includes index.

ISBN 0-88984-189-6

1. Sagas – Translations into English. I. Johnston, George,
1913 Oct. 7 – . II. Bandamanna saga. English. 1999.
III. Viga-Glúm's saga. English. 1999. IV. Title: Viga-Glúm.

PT7269.B4E5   1999   839'.63008   C97-932168-9

Published by The Porcupine's Quill, 68 Main Street, Erin,
Ontario N0B 1T0. Typeset in Perpetua with Celtic Bold
titling. Printed on Zephyr Antique laid, and bound by
The Porcupine's Quill Inc.

The cover and all interior pen-and-ink drawings
are courtesy of Virgil Burnett.

Represented in Canada by the Literary Press Group. Trade
orders are available from General Distribution Services.

We acknowledge the support of the Canada Council for the
Arts for our publishing programme. The support of the
Ontario Arts Council and the Department of Canadian Heritage
through the Book and Periodical Industry Development
Programme is also gratefully acknowledged.

1   2   3   4   •   01   00   99

CONTENTS

MAPS & TABLES

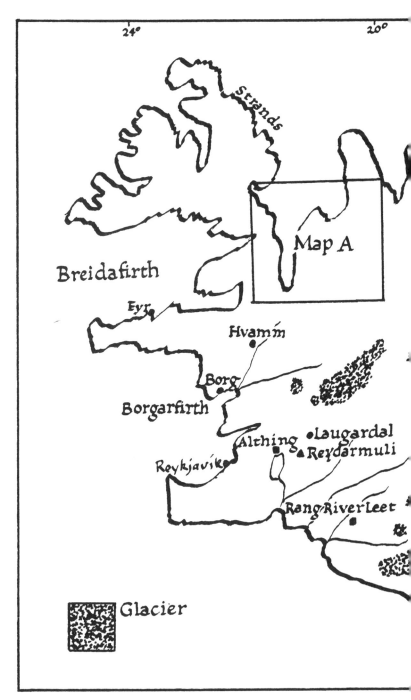

24°   20°

Strands

Map A

Breidafirth

Eyr

Hvamm

Borg

Borgarfirth

Althing ● Laugardal
▲ Reydarmuli

Reykjavik

Rang River Leet

Glacier

Locations defined as 'Map A' and 'Map B' above are detailed
on pages 27 and 79 respectively.

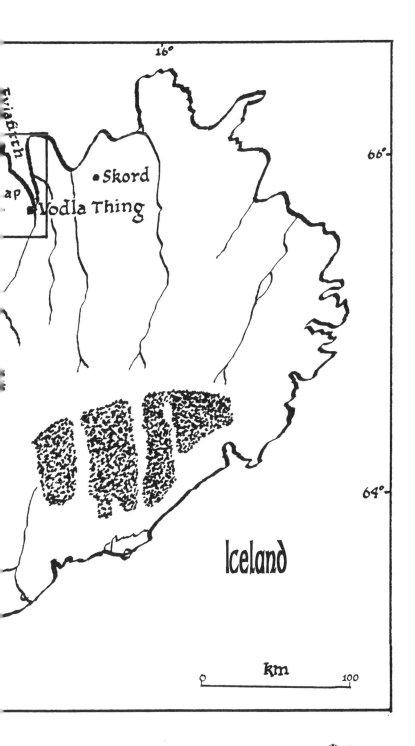

16°

66°

•Skord

Eviabrth

ap

Vodla Thing

64°

Iceland

km

0   100

General Introduction

The two sagas, 'The Schemers' (Bandamanna saga) and 'Viga-Glúm' (Víga-Glúms saga), are included in the kind now known as 'Sagas of Icelanders'. Almost all of these were composed during the thirteenth century in Iceland, and they have become accepted as classics of European literature. The country had then been settled for over three hundred years. 'Sagas of Icelanders', with a very few exceptions, told of named Icelanders who had lived during the early post-settlement period, from the middle of the ninth century to the middle of the eleventh, approximately. They were soberly-told stories, with an air of authenticity, so that they were taken for history until comparatively recently, when scholarship looked at them more closely. They are now recognized as achievements of the story-teller's art, literary in the sense that they were given written form, but composed mostly of orally-preserved stories that had their origins in fact. Some also incorporated folk-tale elements. A few were made up wholly, or all but, in their authors' imaginations.

'The Saga of the Schemers' is one of the few 'Sagas of Icelanders' that must be considered a wholly imaginative work. It is also, in other respects, alone of its kind. It was composed during the high period of saga literature, but unlike any of the rest its mood is comic. Few sagas are without some element of comedy, however fierce it may sometimes be, but they are all weighted on the side of passion and tragedy. Such weight is to be felt in the introductory and closing chapters of 'Schemers', but its central chapters, five of a total of twelve, rise to pure comical satire. Moreover, unlike other sagas, which are predominantly narrative in style, this central portion of 'Schemers' presents itself as drama; it is virtually all dialogue, with just enough unspoken text to set the scenes and move the principals through what action there is.

Its most fully-developed character is Ofeig. He takes charge of the dramatic chapters, handles them his own way, and brings them to a triumphant conclusion. One might conjecture that the author conceived him first, along with his performance at the Althing, and then worked out the chapters that provide the challenge for his performance and the brief denouement that follows. The saga as a whole thus falls into two distinct parts, narrative introduction and denouement being one, and the drama interpolated between them the other. There can be no doubt that the drama is the very reason for the saga's existence; yet its cast of characters, Ofeig included, is self-contained and virtually independent of the beginning and ending, which, considered as a unit, has its own, not inconsiderable, story to tell. Somehow these two separate modes and substances are welded together without apparent transitions. Yet it is not till well into the story, after it has worked itself up to a crisis, that a completely new cast of characters takes over and the action becomes all talk. Then, when this complication has as it were talked itself out, its actors go home and the saga picks up its taciturn narrative again, with its original story line and cast of characters, and comes to a proper conclusion. It is all skilfully done, as though by sleight of hand.

Ofeig is given a second introduction when the narrative has accomplished two thirds of its course and the drama begins to take over. Here, in Chapter 5, he is described as an old man in threadbare and somewhat unusual clothes, walking with a stick, sharp-eyed under his droopy cowl. He appears at the Althing as the improbable rescuer of Odd's case after it has just been quashed in the courts. Odd has already suffered blame for his gullibility at the time of Vali's death, and now he has fumbled his attempt to recover his good name. Ofeig would seem to be an unpromising rescuer, but after taunting his son a little, a game he can never resist, he quickly comes to grips with his problem. He does so in an ironic and morally ambiguous way, first chiding the court for putting aside, on account of a quibble, the truth and justice they have sworn to uphold, and then bribing them with a purse of silver to re-open the case while Odd's opponents are away. The bribery comes to light, and next year at the Althing Odd is faced with the certainty of a charge that will probably result in outlawry and confiscation of his property. There has been a summoning at his farm, and the charge is to be pressed by eight of the most powerful chieftains from the four quarters of the land. At this point Ofeig takes over, and Odd is dismissed from the scene.

It may be said that the eight in the Scheme are worthy of Ofeig. They are distinct individuals, some more fully developed than others, and in differing degrees ill-intentioned, Hermund being the worst. His death is the one supernatural event in the story, and it seems to have been introduced at the end to bear out Egil's prophecy, based on a spaeing, that Hermund would die before him. This has its own irony, for it occurs when Hermund is on his way to burn Egil in his house. He and his confederates are characterized partly by what they do, but mostly by what comes out in

Ofeig's and Egil's exchanges with them. The impulsive Styrmir is the formative genius of the Scheme, Thorarin's sharper wit having first perceived the point of law on which it is based. Thorarin expresses his wisdom in gnomic phrases. He has some kind of nasty habit that Egil derides him for. Hermund is chiefly distinguished by the candour of his greed. Jarnskeggi and Skegg-Broddi are wise enough to hold their tongues, though both are jeered at for their vanity. Thorgeir is made fun of for his stupidity.

We learn about Egil and Gellir from Ofeig's seducing them into his counter-scheme, and also from the different parts they play in it. The first to be approached is Egil. At the beginning of his talk with him Ofeig speaks two verses, as though impromptu, knowing that these will catch the attention of one who himself takes delight in poetry, a near relative and namesake of the great skald, Egil Skallagrimsson. He moves from this to flattery, and to whetting Egil's greed. Then, dramatically withholding his revelation of the sum Egil may expect, he speaks another verse, this time in *dróttkvætt*, the most impressively complex of the Old Norse metrical forms. Ofeig's *dróttkvætt* is both teasing and insulting, as are his account of Odd's response to the scheme, and his own low opinion of the mighty ones who have let themselves be talked into it. It is at this point that he introduces a bag of silver from under his cloak. He again mixes flattery with his scolding and wins Egil over to his counter-scheme. Now he moves off to persuade the shyer bird, Gellir, and he is no longer 'so uncertain in his plan'. He is gentler with him, though he is not above frightening him for his daughter's sake, that Odd might well carry her off if he is outlawed, and burn Gellir's house while he is at it. Would it not be wiser to marry his daughter to Odd's wealth? Ofeig produces his bag of silver as earnest of the dowry that Odd will also provide.

After this comes Ofeig's drama, a kind of sophisticated scolding that might be considered a flyting. It takes place on the lower plain of the Althing site, where he and the Schemers and their men have moved after meeting at the Law Rock. Hermund has agreed in their name that there shall be a settlement out of court provided that the Schemers are granted self-judgement, which is to say that they set their own terms. Settlement out of court virtually lifts the threat of outlawry from Odd. Hermund has also agreed that Ofeig may choose two of their number to set the terms. Thorarin, the coolest and sharpest-witted of them, foresees that he may regret this, but Hermund will not take back his word. When they are seated on the lower plain, Ofeig enters their circle and, making a ceremony of selecting his two, as though he had not already done so, with nice precision and not leaving out Egil and Gellir, he tells them what kind of scoundrels he thinks they are. He concludes with an insulting verse.

Egil is given charge of the second flyting match when he answers the Schemers' outraged questions, and his tongue is quite as sharp as Ofeig's, and bitterer to his confederates, since he had also been one of them. Ofeig completes his triumph with an insulting verse, another *dróttkvætt*. After this, though he has a few more teasing words with Odd and a brief affectionate reunion, his part is over and he leaves the scene.

The introductory and denouement narratives, though they may be secondary to the central drama, have their own considerable weight and involvement. Ospak is a complex villain, conceived by an imagination that in a different saga might have given him a much larger role. But this author had Ofeig waiting in the wings, and he seems more than adequate to taking over, with his comical array of lords to oppose him. Yet Ospak does seem, after the brief denouement, a snubbed potentiality. He shows the same mixed character as his kinsman, Grettir Asmundarson; there is much in him that is capable and helpful, but with it comes a nature and background that most men are unwilling to trust. He brings out both Odd's innocence and Vali's bent for justice, and his villainy, once he is committed to it, is unrepentant. The author must have been rich to have had him to spend so readily. Vali is another who might have filled a larger role in another saga. Even so, his death is pitiable enough for tragedy; he seems almost the sketch for a Baldr.

Viga-Glúm's saga tells the story of a known Icelandic chieftain of the tenth century, Glúm Eyjolfsson, whose first significant public act in Iceland, his killing of Sigmund Thorkelsson on the grain field Vitazgjafi, is noted in *Landnámabók* and the old *Icelandic Annals*. Other events and names in the saga are noted in these sources: the killing of Bard Hallason, for example, and the Hrisateig battle, which latter has been dated as occurring in A.D. 983. Names and events appear in other sagas as well, and genealogies correspond, more or less exactly, with other genealogies. The main story must first have been told, probably in separate episodes, about events that did happen and people who did take part in them. The story cannot, however, be read as history; fictional and folktale motives have been worked into reports of whatever once happened, and supernatural elements, belonging to pagan mythology and worship, have held their place in the story.

The manuscript heading to the saga in *Möðruvallabók* is *Hér hefr Víga-Glúms sögu,* but the byname *Víga*, which means 'of killings', is only added once in the text, and that in the interpolated story about Glúm and Killing-Cavern. In any case his killing of Sigmund was what asserted his standing in the community, and the ensuing law-case at the Althing confirmed it. Supernatural themes that follow conflicting courses through the story were symbolically represented at the killing: on the one side by the cloak, spear and sword that Glúm's maternal grandfather Vigfus had given him, and on the other by the sacred field, Vitazgjafi, on which it took place. Glúm's aggressive and tricky nature, and his confidence, also display themselves here, and his poet's bent for pregnant pronouncements. In the course of the story his confidence proves to be overweening, and the pagan portents and symbols are related to the rise and subsequent decline of his fortunes with an ambiguity whose significance for the author's contemporaries, we cannot expect to more than guess. How much did the author, a Christian in a community that had been Christian for over two hundred years, mean the pagan sanctity of the field to signify? And to what degree did he intend Glúm's confidence and success to follow from his possession of the cloak and spear? If Vitazgjafi was a reliably rich field because it was sacred to the fertility god Frey, whose temple is thought to have overlooked it, then Glúm profaned it and showed his indifference to the god by killing Sigmund on it. The point is given emphasis when Thorkel the tall presents an ox to Frey at his temple and interprets the ox's sudden death as acknowledgement of his gift. At the end of the story, Thorkel's petition seems to be fulfilled. Glúm has a dream of Frey's displeasure. Then he is forced to give up the farm at Thvera and is banished from his district.

In this sequence of events the saga seems to suggest a fatal conflict between the god Frey and Glúm's *gæfa*, the luck and personal force that was passed on to him from Vigfus. Vigfus knew that his *gæfa* was present in his gifts of the cloak and spear, and Glúm acknowledges it again in his grandfather's fetch, who comes to him in his dream. Glúm looked to Vigfus for strength, and turned his back on his paternal ancestor, Helgi the lean, the first settler in the Eyjafirth district, where the saga is located. Helgi was nominally Christian and named his farm Kristnes, but like some others of his time he kept his attachment to the old gods, particularly Thor, in reserve, for situations in which Christianity seemed inadequate. His son Ingjald, Glúm's paternal grandfather, held one of the original priest-chieftaincies in Iceland, and it was probably he who had had the temple to Frey built at Thveraland. The Espihol men were also descended from Helgi the lean through his daughter Ingunn.

Vigfus of Voss, on the other hand, had been a viking who, to judge by his talismans, looked to Odin for his luck, and there are hints in the saga that if Glúm felt attachment to any god it was to Odin. He was a poet, and Odin was the god of poetry; the cloak and spear were Odinic attributes; the name Thunderbenda that he gives to his son, Vigfus, at the Hrisateig battle is a likely name for Odin. His equivocal oath was in Odin's style, and the clothes-drying pole he wants Einar's thralls to raise is recognized by Einar as one to hang them on, and such a hanging would have been a characteristic sacrifice to Odin.

What part do the supernatural signs and figures play in the story? They are not integral. They appear in dreams and symbols but have no direct influence on events. Glúm parts with his cloak and spear as though his confidence is independent of them. † Einar resolves to prosecute Glúm for his equivocal oath when he knows that the tokens of his *gæfa* have been given away, but this decision too may be read as his realization that Glúm has now overreached himself. The turn in Glúm's fortunes had already come when he assigned the killing of Thorvald hook to Gudbrand. There was a kind of justice in the outlawing of Gudbrand, a kind that Halli the stout said was coming to Thorvard. But Glúm's move was too clever, and his punishment for it was harsh.

The author's attitude to the superstitions that belonged to the story would have been ironic. They were probably there from the beginning, but however they came he makes cunning use of them to set off the independence, quirkiness and stoical wisdom of his protagonist.

---

† They are also ambiguous. He would have offended Vigfus of Voss' fetch by giving away the cloak and spear, and his dream would tell him that he had offended Frey. Would he have offended him by swearing two false oaths? At least one of these was sworn in a temple to Frey.

Other stories involving Glúm have been incorporated in the saga, and differences in style suggest that they were not written by the author of the main story. There is reason to suppose that they were introduced in a redaction that was later than the original composition of the saga but earlier than its copying into *Möðruvallabók*. Two obvious and considerable interpolations come in Chapters 13-15, which tell the story of Ingolf† and Barn-Calf, and Chapter 16, which tells of Glúm's encounter with Killing-Cavern. They interrupt the course of the narrative, which seems to break abruptly after Oddbjorg's foretelling of the fateful strife between Steinolf and Arngrim. The story then takes up again, as though the events of the interpolated chapters had not happened. For example, Mar plays a significant part in the Barn-calf episode two chapters before he is formally introduced into the story, along with his brother Vigfus.

Both interpolations are self-contained, and their style is fictional in a way that all but a few parts of the main saga are not. Motives from folklore appear in both, and the verse at the climax of the Killing-Cavern episode seems to belong to other circumstances altogether.

The last two chapters of the saga seem also to have been added after the classical development of the main narrative has been resolved. There is no change of style in these chapters, however, that would make them out of keeping with the rest.

---

† Characters in Ingolf's chapters, except for Glúm, Mar and Einar Konalsson, are found in no other Icelandic writing. Characters in other parts of the saga, on the contrary, are almost all named elsewhere.

The saga tells of one man whose ways and feats impressed themselves on his community strongly, so that his own story lived on, and other stories that typify him attached themselves to it. These stories must have been passed from one teller to another before they were given the form we now have. Glúm comes out in the written saga as a deep one, narrow in his interests and at the same time ruthless and cunning, yet a poet too, and lover of games and deviousness. Turville-Petre refers to him as a peasant. He commands respect, if not affection, and his family loyalty and willingness to help are attractive. The interpolations contribute to our knowledge of his make-up. Ingolf benefits by his helpfulness and also suffers by his crotchetiness, and Killing-Cavern takes advantage of his reliability in a tight corner to trap him. The author does not say that he is a chieftain, nor does he show him sacrificing to Frey; on the contrary, he seems to make a point of his disregard for Frey. Turville-Petre nevertheless asserts that he must have inherited his grandfather Ingjald's *goðorð* because he delivered the twelve-man verdict and had the decisive vote in it. † In Chapter 27 he attempts to consecrate the fall thing, which was a chieftain's duty. The authenticity of this detail in the chapter, however, has been questioned.

Glúm begins life as a conventional hero, slow to develop until he proves himself abroad, which he did against the berserk, Bjorn. His time in Vigfus's hall follows a similar pattern to his father's time in Hreidar's

---

† On twelve-man verdicts and the hallowing of things, see the general note on Law and Government.

house. The laughing fits that signal his killing moods, with their paleness and gushing tears, have the appearance of a convention. His son Vigfus inherits it. It suggests a frightening, more than human dimension to their make-up. In other respects, except for certain details in the interpolations and perhaps Glúm's conversion to Christianity and confirmation, the story is convincing in a matter-of-fact way that, even for a modern reader, is not made less so by the supernatural elements. Glúm's fate was tragic, though he was not hunted down and killed as, for example, Gisli and Grettir were. His downfall was real enough, however, and his overweening confidence brought it on. Emphasis is placed on Glúm's giving away of the cape and spear, but it is his boastful verse that plays his fate into the hands of the malicious clown, Thorvard. Glúm loses his family property and his standing, and has to live out the remainder of his days elsewhere. His story is absorbing because it is a good one, it takes shape and is well told. Many elements of his complex nature are brought out in brief, dramatic scenes: the cool ferocity of his killing of Sigmund, his handling of Gudbrand before and after the battle at Hrisateig, his giving in to Arnor and Vigfus, and ultimately his acceptance of his fate. The manly tissue that his antithetical qualities weave, with their strains and tensions, is convincingly presented. His is a forceful and unpredictable nature to the end.

Textual Information

Earliest copies of both 'The Saga of the Schemers' (Bandamanna saga) and 'The Saga of Viga-Glúm' (Víga-Glúms saga) are preserved in a mid-fourteenth century vellum codex that was given the name *Möðruvallabók* by its seventeenth-century owner, Lawman Magnús Björnsson. It came to Denmark with his son, Sheriff Björn Magnússon, who presented it to the Royal antiquarian, Thomas Bartholin, and from him it passed into Arni Magnússon's library. It is now housed in the Arnamagnæan Institute in Reykjavík, Iceland, with its original code reference, AM 132 fol. It is the most comprehensive single manuscript collection of Icelandic sagas, eleven in all, most of them complete; in some cases these are the only surviving vellum copies. It is therefore of prime critical value.

A second complete vellum text of 'Schemers' is contained in an early fifteenth-century codex from the Old Royal Collection of Denmark, codified as Gl. kgl. saml. 2485 4to. Magerøy considers that this second text, known as K, and the *Möðruvallabók* text M, were based on a common written original, composed probably in the last quarter of the thirteenth century. He regards the M text as in most respects the more faithful copy. He has based his Viking Society edition, from which the present translation has been made, on M, correcting it in a very few places, according to what seemed a better reading in K. Besides these two vellum texts there is a vellum fragment from the latter half of the fifteenth century, and thirty-three still later paper mss., most of them derived from M, but some from K.

William Morris's translation, called 'The Saga of the Banded Men', was published in Morris and Magnússon, 'The Saga Library' Vol. I, London 1891.

The *Möðruvallabók* text of 'Víga-Glúm' is the one early, complete version of the saga. Fragments of late fourteenth-century and early fifteenth-century vellum copyings of the saga are also in the Arnamagnæan Institute in Reykjavík, coded AM 564a 4to and AM 445c 4to. These have been included as appendices in Gabriel Turville-Petre's edition. Many paper copies exist, written in Iceland in the seventeenth and eighteenth centuries; all of these, vellum and paper, stem, directly or indirectly, from *Möðruvallabók*. Turville-Petre dates the composition of the saga in the middle years of the thirteenth century, by a man who knew the Eyjafirth district well, probably a local.

The first printed edition was published at Hólar in Iceland in 1756, the second in Copenhagen in 1786. The second included a Latin translation and notes. An important edition, prepared by Gudmundur Thorláksson, was published in Copenhagen in 1880 as the first volume in the series, *Íslenzkar fornsögur*.

The two most useful editions at present are those of Gabriel Turville-Petre, Oxford, 1940; 2nd edition, 1960, with introduction and notes in English; and Jónas Kristjánsson, *Íslenzk Fornrit* ix, Reykjavík, 1956. Both are currently available.

The first and only English translation until recently was that of Sir Edmund Head, published in London, 1866. Sir Edmund Head was Governor of British North America from 1854 to 1861.

The present translation is based on the Turville-Petre edition. The introduction and notes also owe much to that edition and to Jónas Kristjánsson's introduction and notes.

Chronology

Two events in 'Víga-Glúm' have been given dates in old Icelandic annals: the slaying of Sigmund Thorkelsson on Vitazgjafi, 944, and the battle at *Hrísateigr*, 983. These have been accepted by most scholars as reasonably accurate. At the very end the saga tells us that men say 'that for twenty years Glúm was the mightiest chieftain in Eyjafirth, and for another twenty no-one was better than equal to him'. The twenties are conventionally rounded figures, but the dates nearly enough confirm them. Both Gabriel Turville-Petre and Jónas Kristjánsson are willing to accept these dates as reliable, and they make the dating of Glúm's death at three years after the coming of Christianity to Iceland, which occurred in 1000 A.D., plausible. That he was confirmed on his deathbed by Bishop Kol seems less likely. These dates make the interjected statement at the beginning of Chapter 2, which connects the reign of Hákon Aðalsteinsfóstri, at least by implication, with the beginning of the saga, impossible. Jónas Kristjánsson has calculated Glúm's birth at about 928 in accordance with the annal dates and the saga's date for Glúm's death. This would make his age sixteen or seventeen when he killed Sigmund on Vitazgjafi. Hákon did not come to power until the 930s, or perhaps as late as 946, as more recent scholarship would have it. This must have been at least twelve years after Eyjolf came to Norway, or 28 years, if more recent scholarship is correct.

The Schemers

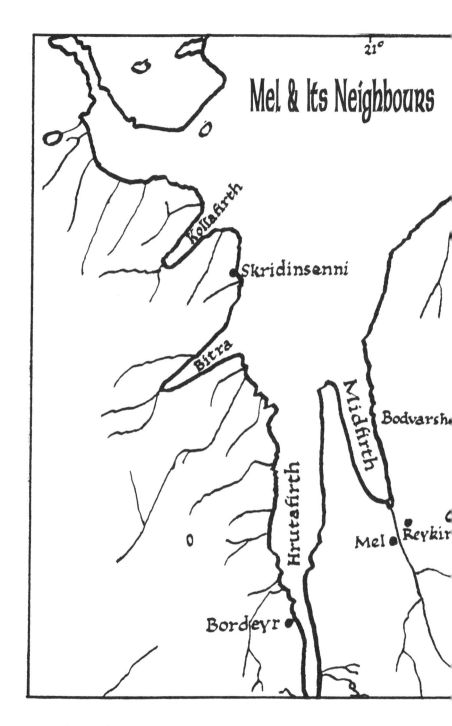

Mel & Its Neighbours

21°

Kollafirth

Skridinsenni

Bitra

Midfirth

Bodvarsh

Hrutafirth

Mel

Reykir

Bordeyr

'Map A', detail – see page 7.

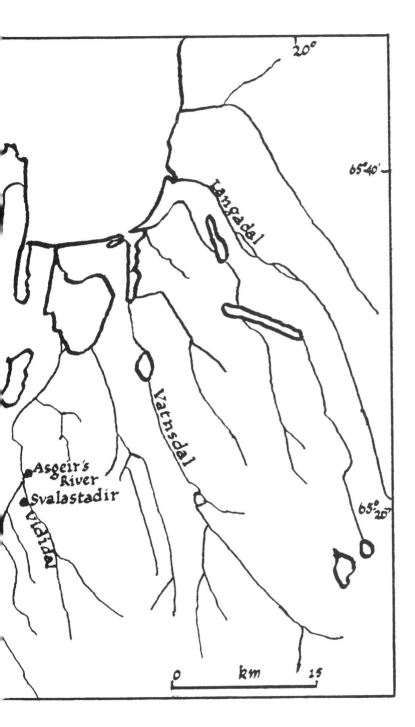

20°

65°40'

Langadal

Vatnsdal

Asgeir's
River
Svalastadir

Vididal

65°
20'

0   km   15

☀ 27

CHAPTER I: There was a man Ofeig who lived west in Midfirth on the farm called Reykir. He was the son of Skidi, and his mother was Gunnlaug; her mother was Jarngerd, daughter of Ofeig Jarngerdsson from Skord, in the north. He was a married man and his wife was Thorgerd, who was daughter of Vali, a woman of good stock and a most capable woman. Ofeig was a very wise man, and the readiest hand for righting difficulties. He was in all ways an outstanding man, but he was not comfortably off, owned much land but did not have much money. To no man was he sparing of food, though his household needs were always hard won. He was thing man of Styrmir of Asgeir's River, who was then the mightiest chieftain in the west there. Ofeig had a son by his wife called Odd, a handsome lad, and from an early age very able. He was not shown much love by his father for he was shy of hard work.

Vali was a man who grew up at home there with Ofeig, a handsome man and well liked. Odd grew up at home with his father till he was twelve years old. For a long while Ofeig had few words for Odd and showed him little affection. The common talk was that no-one there in the district would be abler than Odd, and on a time he comes to speak to his father and asks for an outlay of money: – and I want to go away from here. It is this way, that you set little store by me and neither am I useful in your household.

Ofeig answers: – I shall not make my outlay less than you have earned; I shall make it exact, and you must know how much help that will amount to.

Odd said he could hardly support himself on it, and their talk breaks off.

Next day Odd takes fishing lines from the partition,

☀ 29

all catching tackle and twelve ells of homespun and off he goes then without a good-bye to anyone. He makes for Vatnsness and joins company with fishermen there, and from them he gets help on loan and hire in the way of what he most needs, for when they knew that he came of good stock and was likable himself they venture letting him owe. Now he buys everything on credit, and is with them that year fishing, and it is said that luck was best with those who had Odd in company. He was at this three winters and three summers and had come to the point that he had paid everyone back what he owed them, and had moreover acquired a good sum for himself. Never did he visit his father, and both went on as though neither was kin to the other. Odd was well liked by his fellows.

Next he turns to coasting cargo northwards to the Strands, and he buys a share in a coaster and so acquires some wealth. His wealth grows so quickly that soon he is sole owner of the coaster, and sails this between Midfirth and the Strands a few summers, and by then he is beginning to be well off. It happens as before that he tires of this business. Then he buys into a ship and sails abroad and is on trading voyages for a while, and again he does well at this and is a good merchant; he prospers both in money and standing. He follows this trade till he owns a knarr and the largest part of its cargo, and he carries on with his trading and becomes a very rich man, and noteworthy. He was often with chieftains and men of rank abroad, and was well thought of wherever he stayed. Now he becomes so rich that he has two knarrs on trading voyages; and the saying is that no man trading at that time was as rich as Odd. He was also a luckier seaman than other men; he never made land farther north than Eyjafirth, nor farther west than Hrutafirth.

CHAPTER 2: One summer, as the story tells, Odd brings his ship into Hrutafirth at Bordeyr, intending to be here for the winter. He was urged by his friends, then, to make his home here, and on their entreaty he does so, and buys the land in Midfirth that is called Mel. He sets up a great household there and maintains it in a magnificent way, and it is said that his life there was no less noteworthy than his voyages had been, and now no man was as famous as Odd in all the north of Iceland. He was more openhanded with money than most other men, and a good help in trouble to those who needed him and lived near by; but he never did anything for his father. He laid up his ship in Hrutafirth. It is said that no man was as wealthy here in Iceland as Odd; indeed they do say that he would be as wealthy as three of the wealthiest together. In all kinds his wealth was great, gold and silver, farm lands and livestock. His kinsman Vali was with him while he was here in Iceland and abroad. Odd now lives on his farm and is honoured in the way that has now been told.

The man Glúm is named; he lived at Skridinsenni; that is between Bitra and Kollafirth. He was married to the woman Thordis; she was daughter of Asmund greylocks, father of Grettir Asmundarson. Ospak was the name of their son. He was a big build of a man and strong, hard to deal with and arrogant; he was soon in the coasting trade between the Strands and the north districts; an able man and a brute in strength. One summer he came into Midfirth and sold his goods, and then, on a day, he got himself a horse and rode up to Mel and meets Odd. They exchanged compliments and the common news.

Ospak spoke: – It is this way, Odd, said he, that good words are spoken about your householding; you are much praised by men, and all think themselves well placed who are with you. Now I expect that it will prove the same for me; I should like to come in here with you.

Odd answers: – Men do not praise you much, and your friends are few; you are thought to have slyness up your sleeve, you come by that from your kin.

Ospak answers: – Stand by your own trial, and not what others say, for 'Not much is gilded in the telling'. I am not asking for gifts; I would have room from you, but provide my own keep, and you see how you feel about it then.

Odd answers: – You and your kin are powerful, and ugly if it suits you to turn against someone, but since you challenge me to accept you, then we may both chance it for a winter.

Ospak receives this with thanks, moves himself and his goods to Mel in the fall, and from the first he is faithful to Odd, serves him well about the farm and does the work of two men. Odd is much pleased with him. Winter passes, and when spring comes Odd bids him stay on, says it would seem best so. This is now Ospak's wish too, and he keeps busy about the farm, and it prospers famously. Folk think it a wonder, how this man has turned out. He is not only liked for himself, but the farm as well fairly blooms, and no man's state seems worthier than Odd's, which seems to lack only one thing to achieve full honour, as people think: that he does not have a chieftaincy. It was a common practice at that time for men to assume a new chieftaincy, or purchase one, and this is what Odd did.

Thing men soon gathered about him; all were keen to join him. And now it is quiet for a time.

CHAPTER 3: Odd thinks well of Ospak, lets him have a large hand in the managing. He was a skilful worker and willing worker too, the right man for the farm. Winter passes, and Odd is still better pleased with Ospak than before, because he takes on more. In the fall he rounds up the sheep from the fells, and it proved a good round-up, not a sheep missing. Now the next winter passes and spring comes. Odd makes it known that he intends going abroad in summer, and says that his kinsman Vali is to take over the managing.

Vali answers: — It is this way, kinsman, that I am not used to such work, and I will rather look after our money and merchandise.

Odd now turns to Ospak and bids him take over the farm.

Ospak answers: — That is too much for me, though things go well now, while you are at hand.

Odd keeps on, and Ospak demurs, though he would mad eagerly have it; and it comes to the point that he bids Odd decide, if he promises him his care and confidence. Odd says he is to manage his property in such a way as to become as well set and popular as could be; says he has learned that no other man could manage his property with a better will or understanding. Ospak then agrees that it shall be as he decides. So ends their talk. Odd readies his ship and has cargo brought to it.

This becomes known and is much discussed.

Odd needed no long readying. Vali is to go with him. Then, when he is quite ready, men see him down to the ship. Ospak went a longer way with him; they had much to talk about and when they were almost at the ship Odd spoke: –

Now there is this one thing that has not been decided.

What is that? said Ospak.

Nothing has been seen to about my chieftaincy, said Odd, and I want you to take it over.

That will not do at all, says Ospak. I am not up to that. I have already taken more in hand than I am likely to manage or carry out well. There is no man so apt for this as your father; he is the fittest man for lawsuits, and very wise.

Odd says that he will not put it in his hands: – and I want you to take it over.

Ospak demurs, and yet he would gladly have it.

Odd says he will be angry if he does not accept, and at their parting Ospak does take over the chieftaincy.

Odd now sails abroad and his voyage speeds well, as it always did for him.

Ospak goes home, and there was much talk about this business. Odd is thought to have put a good deal of authority in this man's hands. Ospak rides to the Thing in summer with a body of men, and carries out his part ably, understands what the law expects of him, fulfils that well and rides from the Thing with honour. He supports his men firmly, they are never put down, and not much is tried against them, and he is ready and helpful towards all his neighbours. Nor does there seem to be any less array or open-handedness about the farm than before. Care is not stinted and such husbandry prospers.

Now summer passes. He rides to the Leet and

hallows it; and at harvest's end he goes to the fells when men are after the dry sheep, and his round-up is a good one, it is thoroughly followed through, not a sheep is missing, of his or Odd's either.

CHAPTER 4: It happened in the fall that Ospak came north into Vididal to Svalastadir; the woman Svala was householding there. He was received graciously. She was a handsome woman and young. She talks with Ospak and asks if he will see to her husbandry: — I have heard that you are a great manager.

He was pleased by this, and their talk grows lively; they take a liking to each other and look close at each other, and friendly, and their talk comes round to his asking who has the say about her marrying.

No man of any standing is nearer kin to me, she says, than Thorarin Langdalers' Chieftain, the wise.

Then Ospak rides to meet Thorarin and there he is received without warmth. He puts forward his errand and asks for Svala.

Thorarin answers: — I can not be eager for kinship with you. There is much talk about your doings. I know this, that there are no halfway measures with such folk, it is either lift her stock and have her fetched here, or the pair of you do as you please. Now, I shall have no part of it, and I call it not my affair.

After this Ospak rides away and comes to Svalastadir and tells her how it stands. They make a marriage between them then, and on her own she betroths herself and moves with him to Mel, and they keep the farm at Svalastadir and have men there to run it. Now Ospak is at Mel, and he kept up a high style in his householding; yet he was thought a very hard man to deal with.

Winter passes, and in summer Odd arrived back out in Hrutafirth. He had again prospered in money and fame. He comes home to Mel, looks over his possessions and is pleased that they seem well kept up. Now summer passes. One day Odd says to Ospak that it would be right for him to take back his chieftaincy.

Ospak spoke: – Ay, says he, that is the thing I was least eager to agree to and least fit for, and I am quite ready for this, but I think men are most used to its being done at leets or at things.

Odd answers: – That may well be.

Summer wears on to the Leet. And on the morning of the Leet when Odd wakes up he looks about and sees few men in the sleeping room. He has slept soundly and long. He sprang up and saw that men were quite gone from the room. He thought this strange, but said little; he gets ready, and a few men with him, and they ride to the Leet. A crowd of men were there before them when they arrived, and they were mostly ready to leave, and the Leet had been hallowed. Odd's eyebrows go up, he thinks this turn of events very strange.

Men ride home, and some days pass.

It was again one day that Odd sat at table and Ospak across from him, and when least expected Odd springs from the table at Ospak and has a raised axe in his hand, tells him to make over the chieftaincy now.

Ospak answers: – You need not be so fierce about asking; have back the chieftaincy when you will. I did not know you would be serious about it.

He then reached forth his hand and made over the chieftaincy to Odd.

There was quiet then for a while, and henceforth little went on between the two, Odd and Ospak. Ospak is rather surly in their exchanges. Men suspect that Ospak would have meant the chieftaincy for himself and not Odd if it had not been cowed from him in such a way that he could not avoid yielding it. Now nothing is done in the way of farm management; Odd calls on him for nothing, nor is there talk between them about it. Then comes a day when Ospak gets ready to go. Odd carries on as though he is not aware; they part without either acknowledging the other. Ospak rides to Svalastadir to his farm. Odd behaves as though nothing has happened and it is quiet now, the while.

This is told, that in the fall men go up on the fells and Odd's round-up comes far short of what it had been. He missed forty wethers this time and all were among the best of his flock; they are hunted far and wide over the fells and moors and not found. This was thought very unusual, for Odd seemed to be lucky with his livestock beyond other men. Such great effort was put into the search that it was carried into other districts as well as near home, and to no avail. And at last even this flags, and yet there was much talk about how it might have happened.

Odd was glum during the winter. Vali, his kinsman, asked him why he should be glum: – or do you make so much of the disappearance of the wethers? Your ship cannot be riding steady if such things grieve you.

Odd answers: – I do not grieve that I have lost the wethers. What seems worse to me is that I do not know who stole them.

Does it seem certain to you, says Vali, that that is what happened, and if so, whom do you most suspect?

Odd answers: – There is no hiding that I think Ospak stole them.

Vali answers: — Your friendship has altered now from what it was when you set him over all your goods.

Odd said it had been the worst kind of blunder, and might well have turned out worse.

Vali said: — Most folk spoke of it as a wonder. Now I wish you would not twist the matter so suddenly to blaming him; the risk in words is that they may come to seem hasty. I should like us to agree on this, said Vali, that you let me manage how it is to be done and I shall get to the truth.

They make the agreement.

Vali readies his journey and rides out with his wares into Vatnsdal and Langadal and sells some goods. He was a helpful man, and well liked. He rides on his way till he comes to Svalastadir, and there he was given a good welcome. Ospak was in high spirits.

Vali got ready to leave in the morning. Ospak went beyond the close with him and asked much about Odd. Vali spoke well of his affairs. Ospak praised him and said he was a most generous man: — but did he not suffer losses last fall?

Vali said it was so.

What guesses are there about the disappearance of the sheep? Odd has always been lucky with his stock till now.

Vali answers: — There is more than one opinion about that. Some think it was man's doing.

Ospak says: — That seems improbable, not many are up to such trickery.

As you say, says Vali.

Ospak spoke: — Does Odd make any guess about it?

Vali spoke: — He says little about it, but there is much talk among other folk as to how it might have happened.

That is to be expected, said Ospak.

It is this way, said Vali, since we have spoken of it, that some think it not unlikely to have been your doing. They put it together that you two broke off abruptly and the disappearance came not long after.

Ospak answers: − I would not have expected to hear such a thing from you, and if we were not such friends I would bring it down hard on you.

Vali answers: − There is no need for you to deny it or get so fired up about it. I have looked over your stores here and there can be no question that you have acquired much more than is likely to have come your way honestly.

Ospak answers: − That is not how it is, as will be found, and I wonder how our enemies talk if friends say such things.

Vali answers: − I am not saying this to you unfriendly, however, since you are the only one to hear. Now, if you do as I wish and own up to me, you will be let off easy, for I shall offer a plan. I have sold my goods all around in the district. I shall say that you have got some from me and bought meat and other goods; no-one will disbelieve that. I shall make it that no disgrace comes your way if you follow my plan.

Ospak says that he will not own up to it.

Then worse will happen, says Vali, and no-one but yourself to blame.

They separate then, and Vali rides home.

Odd asks what he had found out about the sheep vanishing.

Vali let on that he had learned little.

Odd spoke: − There is no need to hide it, that Ospak did the stealing, for you would be glad to clear him if you could.

It is quiet now over the winter. And when spring and the summoning days come Odd rides out with twenty men till he was hard by the close at Svalastadir. Then Vali spoke to Odd: —

You bait your horses while I ride to the house and speak to Ospak, see if he will come to terms, and the case need go no further.

They do so, and Vali rides to the house. No-one was outside; doors were open; Vali goes in; it was dark in the house. And when least expected a man leaps up from the wall bench and strikes Vali between the shoulders so that he fell straightway down. It was Ospak.

Vali spoke: — Take yourself off, unlucky man, for Odd is just beyond the close and means to kill you. Send your wife to him and have her say that we have agreed between us and you have owned up to the charge, and I have ridden on my money-collecting out in the dales.

Then Ospak spoke: — This is the worst deed; I meant it for Odd and not you.

Now Svala meets Odd and says that Ospak and Vali have agreed between them: — and Vali bade you turn back.

Odd believes this and rides home.

Vali died and his body was brought to Mel. For Odd these were heavy tidings, and ill. There was dishonour for him on account of it, and things seemed to have taken a black turn. Now Ospak vanishes away so that no-one knows what has become of him.

CHAPTER 5: Now it is to be told that Odd readies the case for the Thing, and names a panel of neighbours from home. It happens that a man dies whom he had named. Odd names another in his stead. Now men ride to the Thing and it is quiet there till the courts sit. And when the courts go to their places Odd brings forward the case for manslaughter, and he does that with ease, and now a defence is called for A little apart from the courts sat the chieftains, Styrmir and Thorarin, with their men.

Then Styrmir spoke to Thorarin: — Now a defense is called for in the manslaughter case, and will you make some answer to this charge?

Thorarin answers: — I shall have no part in it, for I think Odd has need enough to prosecute for such a man as Vali was, and against one whom I take to be the worst of men.

Ay, said Styrmir, no good man is he to be sure, and yet you are somewhat answerable for him.

I care nothing about that, said Thorarin.

Styrmir spoke: — On the other hand there is this to consider, that there will be trouble for you, and more so and more difficult if he is outlawed. I think it is worth pondering, and let us look for a way out, for we can both see a defense for the charge.

I saw that long ago, says Thorarin, and yet I think it not wise to interfere.

Styrmir spoke: — It bears heaviest on you, however, and men will say that you have become poor-spirited if the charge carries and the defense is plain to be seen. And the very truth is that it would be well if Odd were to know that others are worth something and not only he. He·treads us and our thing men all under foot so that the talk is of no-one but him; no harm if he were to find out how learned in the law he is.

Thorarin answers: — You shall have your way, and I

shall support you; but it does not promise well, and it will have a bad ending.

We cannot go by that, said Styrmir. He springs up, walks to the court and asks what stage they were at in their proceedings.

He was told what.

Styrmir spoke: – It so happens, Odd, that a defense has been found in your case. You have made it up wrong, you have called ten neighbours at home; that is not lawful; you should have called them here at the Thing and not in the district. Now either you leave the court as the case stands or we shall bring forward the defense.

Odd says nothing and ponders the matter, concludes that they are correct, goes from the court with his men and back to his booth. And as he comes to the booth lane a man is advancing towards him, an aged man. He is wearing a black sleeve-cloak and it was threadbare; there was only one sleeve in the cloak and it was sticking out at the back. He had a staff in his hand with a point to it, wore a droopy cowl, peered out sharp-eyed from under it, jabbed downwards with his staff and went rather bowed. It was gaffer Ofeig had come, his father.

Then Ofeig spoke: – You come early from the court, said he, and you are gifted in more ways than one if everything goes so swift and sure for you. But what then, is that Ospak outlawed?

No, said Odd, he is not outlawed.

Ofeig spoke: – It is not good manners to fool an old man like me; but how can he be not outlawed? Was he not guilty as charged?

Guilty indeed, says Odd.

How then? says Ofeig; I thought there must be teeth in the charge, for was he not slayer of Vali?

No-one denies that, says Odd.

Ofeig spoke: — Why is he not outlawed, then?

Odd answers: — A defense was found against the charge, and it fell to the ground.

Ofeig spoke: — How could a defense be found against such a rich man's charge?

They called it wrong for the panel to be made up in the district, says Odd.

Impossible, when it was you who had charge of the case, said Ofeig. But perhaps you are better fitted for money-making and voyages than for the proper handling of cases at law. And yet I think that you are not telling me the truth.

Odd answers: — I care never a whit whether you believe me or not.

That may be so, said Ofeig, yet I knew as soon as you went from the district that the case was wrongly prepared; but you thought you were able to do it all on your own and would not ask advice of anyone, and now you think yourself sufficient for this matter too. It may go well for you now, but more likely it will prove difficult for one who thinks everyone beneath him.

Odd answers: — It is clear at any rate that no help may be expected from you.

Ofeig spoke: — The only help in your case will be to make use of me in it; but how sparing of money would you be if one were to set it right?

Odd answers: — I would not be sparing at all, if there might be help in the matter.

Ofeig spoke: — Then let you put a fat purse in this old man's hands, for many eyes will squint after money.

Odd gives him a fat purse.

Then Ofeig asked: — Was the legal defense put forward or not?

We left the court first, said Odd.

Ofeig answers: — That is the only advantage we have, what you did unwitting.

They part now, and Odd goes back to his booth.

CHAPTER 6: The story continues that gaffer Ofeig walks up on to the fields and to the courts, comes to the Northlanders' Court and asks what might be going forward there in men's cases. He is told that some have been judged and some readied for summing up.

At what stage is my son Odd's case, or is that one closed now?

Closed as may be, they said.

Ofeig spoke: — Has he been outlawed, that Ospak?

No, they say, he has not.

How has that come about? said Ofeig.

A defense was found against the charge, said they, for it was wrongly prepared.

Ay, said Ofeig, said he, will you approve my coming into the court?

They do so.

He goes into the court ring and sits himself down.

Ofeig spoke: — Has my son Odd's case been judged?

Judged it has, as may be, they say.

What does that mean? says Ofeig. Did the charge go astray against Ospak? Did he not kill Vali without cause? Was this against it, that there was some doubt in the charge?

They say: — A defense was found against the charge, and it fell to the ground.

How did that defense go? said Ofeig.

He was told.

So indeed, says he. Do you consider it any kind of justice that you heed such worthless considerations and do not sentence the worst kind of man outlaw, a thief and killer? Is it not a weighty matter to find a man not guilty who is worthy of death, and so judge in defiance of justice?

They said that it did not seem right, and yet, they said, it was what was laid upon them.

It may be so, said Ofeig.

Did you swear the oath? says Ofeig.

To be sure, said they.

So you must have, said he, but what did you swear to in words? Was it not this, that you would judge according to what you knew to be truest and justest and most lawful? This is what you would swear.

They agreed that it was so.

Then Ofeig spoke: – But what truer and juster sentence could there be than that the worst kind of man be outlawed and killed and denied all aid, one who has been proved guilty of theft and, moreover, of killing the unoffending man, Vali? But there is a third thing covered by the oath that may be called somewhat awry. Think now for yourselves which is worth more, those two words that concern truth and justice, or that one other which concerns the law. It will surely be apparent to you, for you must have the wit to see the heavy responsibility in judging a man free who is deserving of death when you have sworn oaths that you would judge according to what you know to be most just. You may well believe that it will bear heavily on you, for you will hardly clear yourselves of responsibility.

Ofeig from time to time lets the purse slip down from under his cloak, and from time to time he pulls it up. He observes that their eyes follow the purse.

Then he spoke to them: – It would be wiser to judge rightly and truly, as you have sworn, and have the thanks and good will of prudent and just men for doing so.

He then took the purse and, shaking the silver out, counted it before them.

Now I would do you a friendly turn, said he, and yet I see more for you in my plan than for myself; and I do so because some of you are my friends and some kinsmen, and yet only such as are needy and must each look out for himself. I shall give every man who sits in this court an ounce of silver, and to him who sums up the case I shall give four ounces, and in that way you have money and clear yourselves of responsibility too, and do not break your oaths, which is most important of all.

They ponder the matter, and the truth seems to be in his arguments; they think they have already got into a bad corner over the oath-breaking and they choose the way out that Ofeig has offered them.

Odd is then sent for and he comes, and the two chieftains, Styrmir and Thorarin, have already gone back to their booths. The case is now brought forward and Ospak is made outlaw, and thereupon witnesses are named to attest that the verdict has been given. This accomplished, the men go back to their booths.

There was no rumour of this during the night, and at the Law Rock in the morning Odd stands up and proclaims in a loud voice: – A man was outlawed here last night, Ospak by name, in the Court of the

Northlanders, for the killing of Vali. And this is to be said of his outlaw marks, that he is a big-built man and bold; he has brown hair and the bones of his face are big; black eyebrows, big hands, stout legs, and altogether his stature is extraordinarily big, and he is the most criminal looking of men.

Eyebrows now go up mightily. Many had had no earlier intelligence of this, and it now appears that Odd has followed it up hard, and luck must have been with him, considering the state his case had got into.

CHAPTER 7: It is said that Styrmir and Thorarin have a talk about it.

Styrmir spoke: – We have suffered much shame and dishonour from this case.

Thorarin agreed that it did seem so: – and sharp-witted men have been at work here.

Ay, said Styrmir, do you see any way of setting it right, now?

I cannot see that it will be done quickly, says Thorarin.

What is to be done, then? says Styrmir.

Thorarin answers: – There would be a charge in it, that money was brought into the court, and that would have teeth.

Then it does look promising, supposing we can put it right, says Styrmir.

Off they go, then, and back to their booths.

They call their friends and kindred-in-law together for a deliberation. First was Hermund Illugason, second Gellir Thorkelsson, third Egil Skulason, fourth Jarnskeggi Einarsson, fifth Skegg-Broddi Bjarnason, sixth Thorgeir Halldoruson and the two, Styrmir and Thorarin. These

eight men settle down to deliberate. Styrmir and
Thorarin recount the unfolding of the case and tell how
it stands, and what a great windfall Odd's wealth would
be, they would all live in plenty from it. They draw up
a fast agreement between them that they will support
each other in the scheme, so that from it will come
either a sentence or self-judgement. After this they bind
themselves with oaths, such as they think will not be
budged, and no-one will have the confidence or the
knowledge to stand against them. This agreed, they part,
and men ride home from the Thing, and at first the
scheme is kept quiet.

After the winter father and son meet at the hot
springs and Ofeig asks for the news. Odd says he has
heard none, and asks in his turn. Ofeig says that Styrmir
and Thorarin have mustered men and intend a
summoning ride to Mel. Odd asks what the object of
this would be, and Ofeig tells him the whole of their
intent.

Odd answers: – This does not seem weighty to me.

Ofeig says: – Perhaps it will not prove beyond your
strength.

Time leads on to the summoning days, and along
come Styrmir and Thorarin to Mel with a crowd of
men, and Odd had many men to face them. They
publish their charge and summon Odd to the Althing on
account of his having had money brought into the court
unlawfully. Nothing more happens worth telling, and
they ride away with their following. Then again it
happens that father and son meet and have a talk. Ofeig
asks if he still thinks it amounts to nothing.

Odd answers: – The charge does not seem weighty to
me.

To me it seems otherwise, says Ofeig, but how fully do you grasp the state it has got into?

Odd said he knew what had happened so far.

Ofeig answers: – There will be more heft in it yet, that is my view, because six other chieftains, of the mightiest, have come into it with them.

Odd answers: – They seem to think it needs much.

Ofeig spoke: – What will your plan be now?

Odd answers: – What but ride to the Thing and seek support?

Ofeig answers: – That would seem unpromising to me, with the turn matters have taken. It will not be good to let honour depend on the support of numbers.

What is to do, then? says Odd.

Ofeig answers: – I would advise you to ready your ship while the Thing is on, and be freighted with all your movable goods before men ride away from it. And now, which would you think is better placed, money they take from you, or what is in my hands?

It would seem not so bad if you have it.

Then Odd gives his father a fat purse full of silver, and they go their separate ways. Odd readies his ship and gets a crew for it. Time leads on to the Thing, and the plan goes forward quietly, so that few have any sure intelligence of it.

CHAPTER 8: Now the chieftains ride to the Thing and make a great crowd. Gaffer Ofeig was in Styrmir's following. Schemers Egil and Gellir and Styrmir and Hermund and Thorarin agreed to meet on Blaskog Moor and ride together south to the plain of the Thing. Skegg-Broddi and Thorgeir Halldoruson from Laugardal ride from the East, and Jarnskeggi from the North, and meet at Reydarmuli. They all ride down then to the plains and so to the Thing. Most of the talk there is about Odd's case. All are of one mind, that there will be no-one to answer for him; they think that few would dare attempt, much less be likely to achieve, anything, such great ones as would have to be faced. To the chieftains everything seems prosperous about their case, and they swagger mightily, nor is there a man to throw in a word against them.

Odd had asked no-one to stand for his case. He readies his ship in Hrutafirth when men had ridden to the Thing.

It was one day that gaffer Ofeig went from his booth, and he was much troubled in his mind; sees not a man who might be of his party and thought the weight against him much to challenge; can hardly imagine his lone-handed course against such chieftains, and in a case for which there could be no legal defence; goes bent-kneed as he wanders, tottering, among the booths; carries on like this a long while and fetches up at last at Egil Skulason's booth. Men were there who had come to talk with Egil. Ofeig stepped up by the booth door and waited till the men had gone away. Egil saw them off, and when he is about to go back in Ofeig comes up to him and greeted him. Egil looked at him and asked who he might be.

Ofeig is my name, said he.

Egil spoke: — Are you the father of Odd?

He said it was so.

Then you will want to talk about his case, and there is no need to talk about that with me; much more has already been done about it than I can add anything to. Others too are deeper into the case than I; Styrmir and

❈ 50

Thorarin; they take most of it on themselves, though we support them in it.

Ofeig answers, and a verse took shape in his mouth:

> No honour now
> to name my son;
> not a mention
> make of him here:
> little knows he
> of law, the noddy,
> though of wealth
> wields he full store.

and he spoke another:

> Happy is this
> old homebody
> most to word it
> with witty lads;
> you will not grudge me
> the gift of talk,
> wise you are called
> by worthy men.

I can find other pastime than going on about Odd's business; that has been more prosperous than it is now. But you will not want to deny me some talk; it is the best kind of pastime for an old fellow to talk with such men and so spend a while.

Egil answers: — I shall not refuse you a talk.

They go together now and sit down. Then Ofeig begins: —

Are you a farming man, Egil?

He agreed that he was.

Are you householding there at Borg?

I am, says Egil.

Ofeig spoke: — I hear good things about you, and much to my mind. I am told that you are not stingy of food with any man and you make a brave show, and things have gone a not dissimilar way for us two, both of good birth and openhanded, but in difficulties about money; and I am told that you are glad to help your friends.

Egil answers: — I should be well pleased if I were spoken of as you are, for I know that you are well-born and wise.

Ofeig spoke: — In this, however, we are not alike, that you are a mighty chieftain and fear nothing, whatever lies ahead, and never give ground whoever you have to do with, but I am humble. Yet our bents are much alike, and it is a great pity that such men should be somewhat short of money who are so lofty in spirit.

Egil answers: — That may soon change, so that life will be easier.

How will that come about? said Ofeig.

I see it this way, said Egil: if we take over Odd's property we shall lack little, for we are told great things about that wealth.

Ofeig answers: — It would be no overstatement to call him the richest man in Iceland; and yet you will be curious to know what your share of the money will turn out to be, for you are much in need of it.

That is the truth, said Egil, and a good old one you are, and wise, and you must know to the last ounce what Odd's wealth amounts to.

He answers: — I undertake that it is not better known

to anyone than it is to me, and I can tell you that no-
one calls it so much that it will not be much more.
Nevertheless I have reckoned up what your portion of it
will be. And a verse took shape in his mouth: —

> Truly eight gold tricksters
> trust gain before justice;
> good faith left regardless,
> gone the wealth-gods' honour;
> gold would I most gladly
> grudge you eight curmudgeons;
> honour too; may only
> all disgrace befall you.

What? A likely thing! says Egil. But you are a right
scald.

Ofeig spoke: — I shall not keep from you what plenty
you will come into, and that is the sixteenth part of
Melsland.

Hear a wonder! said Egil. But how can that be? The
wealth is not as great as I thought, then.

Ofeig answers: — Not so, the wealth is very great;
nevertheless, this is very nearly what I expect you will
get. Have you not reckoned that you should get the half
of Odd's wealth between you, and the men of the
Quarter the other half? Then I calculate it thus: if you
are eight in the scheme, yourself will have the sixteenth
part of Melsland; for you must have meant that and
agreed on that. You have taken this up more
scandalously than there can be any precedent for, yet
this must be what you intended. Or did you have some
expectation that my son Odd would sit quiet in the face
of your overweening when you rode north there? No,

said Ofeig, Odd will not be at a nonplus on account of you, and however great his store of wealth, he is no less well supplied with gumption and stratagems when he thinks these are needed. And I would guess that his knarr will glide as sweetly under him on the Iceland sea for all that you call him outlaw. But how can it be considered outlawry that has been so wrongfully taken up? It will fall on them that are pressing it, and I undertake that he will now be afloat with all he owns except the land at Mel — he means that for all of you. He has heard that it is no long path up to Borg from the shore if he sails into Borgarfirth. Now this will end the same way it was begun, for shame and disgrace is what you will win by it, and well deserved, and every man's blame to boot.

Then Egil said: — This must be daylight truth, and now there are sharp wits at work. It was much more likely that Odd would not sit feckless about it, and I shall not fault him for that, for there are some in the scheme whom I gladly wish dishonour from it, and who press hardest for it, such as Styrmir, or Thorarin and Hermund.

Ofeig spoke: — It will go a better way, and that way will be more fitting, for many will blame them for this. But it would seem poor to me if your lot from it proves to be a slim one, for I like you well enough, and indeed the best of you Schemers.

He now lets a fat purse slip down under his cloak.

Egil's eye was caught.

Ofeig marks that, pulls the purse up as quick as he can under his cloak, and spoke: — So it is, Egil, says he, that I expect it to go very nearly as I have told you. Now I shall honour you with something.

He pulls out the purse and pours the silver into the skirt of Egil's cloak; it was two hundred of the best silver known: – This you shall have from me if you do not go against my plan, and it will be a little token of esteem.

Egil answers: – I can see that you are no middling wicked old man; you need not expect that I shall be willing to break my oath.

Ofeig says: – You are not what you think you are, the lot of you. You want to be known as chieftains, but have no notion of what is best for you when you get into some difficulty. You must not take it up wrong, for I shall put the very plan to you that will let you keep to your oath.

What plan is that? said Egil.

Ofeig spoke: – Have you not all agreed that you should have a conviction or else self-judgement?

Egil said it was so.

It is possible, said Ofeig, that we kinsmen of Odd will be let choose which it is to be. Now it may happen that the award will be on your decision. Then I want you to keep it moderate.

Egil answers: – You speak the truth, and you are a cunning old fellow and wise, and yet I am not ready for this, having neither the might nor the men to stand alone against all these chieftains, for there is bound to be ill will if anyone opposes them.

Ofeig spoke: – How then if another comes into the plan with you?

Then it would come nearer, said Egil.

Ofeig spoke: – Which would you have me choose before others in the scheme? Speak as though I had choice of them all.

Two are at hand, said Egil. Hermund is my nearest neighbour, and there is bad feeling between us, but another is Gellir, and I shall choose him.

That is much to grant, says Ofeig, for I wish them all an ill outcome of this case except only you. But he will have the wit to see which is the better choice, to have money and honour, or do without the money and have dishonour too. So now, will you agree to the plan, if it comes under you, to keep the award small?

I shall, to be sure, said Egil.

Then let this be firm between us, said Ofeig, for I shall be back with you very soon.

CHAPTER 9: Now Ofeig goes away, and he and Egil part. Ofeig wanders among the booths, dragging his feet, but he is not so downhearted in himself as feeble of foot, and not so loose-gripped on affairs as laboured in gait. At last he comes to the booth of Gellir Thorkelsson and asks to have him called out. He comes forth and greets Ofeig first, for he was a modest man, and asks what his errand may be.

Ofeig answers: – It is just that I have been wandering this way.

Gellir spoke: – You will be wanting to talk about Odd's case.

Ofeig answers: – I have no desire to talk about that, for I think myself well clear of it, and I am for other pastime.

Gellir spoke: – What would you talk about, then?

Ofeig spoke: – I am told that you are a wise man, and it is a pleasure for me to talk with wise men.

They sit themselves down for a talk between them.

Then Ofeig asks: – What younger men are there in

the west that you think likely to become great chieftains?

Gellir said that there was good choice of such men, and names the sons of Snorri the chieftain and the men of Eyr.

I have been told, said Ofeig, that there would be, and indeed I have come to the right one to ask, since I am talking with a man who is both truthful and frank. But now, who are the best matches among the women there in the west?

He names the daughters of Snorri the chieftain and the daughters of Steinthor of Eyr.

I hear tell of them, said Ofeig. But how, then, do you not have daughters?

Gellir said that he did indeed.

Why do you not name them? said Ofeig. None can be fairer than your daughters, if likeness has anything to do with it. But are they not married?

They are not, said he.

How comes that? said Ofeig.

Gellir says: – Because no-one has courted them who has great wealth and a good homestead, comes of a mighty family and is a proper man himself. Well off I may not be, yet I shall be careful in my choice for the sake of my high kinship and honour. And now, you shall not be let ask all the questions. What men in the north give promise of becoming chieftains?

Ofeig answers: – There is good choice of men. First I count Einar, son of Jarnskeggi, and then Hall Styrmisson. Some men say too that my son Odd is a promising man; and now I shall repeat to you his own words, as he asked me to do, that he would wish to become your kinsman and marry that daughter of yours, Ragnheid.

Ay, said Gellir, said he, time was when that would have been given a good answer, but the way things are I guess it will be put off.

How comes that? said Ofeig.

Gellir spoke: – A cloud seems to hang over your son Odd's affairs, the way things are.

Ofeig answers: – I tell you truly that you will never marry her better than with him, for everyone will agree that he is as accomplished as the very best, and moreover he lacks neither money nor good kin; and you are much in need of money, and it might so happen that you would be given support by him, for he is openhanded to his friends.

Gellir says: – It might be considered if this lawsuit did not stand over him.

Ofeig answers: – Forget that nonsense, it is worthless, a shame and downright foolishness on the part of those in it.

Gellir answers: – Nevertheless it is not less likely to go otherwise, so I shall not agree. And yet if this difficulty might be resolved I should welcome the match eagerly.

Ofeig answers: – It may work out, Gellir, that you will all come into plenty through this; and yet I can tell you what your share of it will be, because I know all about it, and at best reckoning you eight in the scheme will divide the half of Melsland among you. And your share will not be good, you will have got little money and lost your name for honesty and honourable dealing, you who have always been called one of the most honourable in the land.

Gellir asked how it might turn out so.

Ofeig answers: – I think it most likely that Odd is

now at sea with all he owns except the land at Mel. You would not expect him to be at a nonplus over this and let you play at divide and deal among you. No, said Ofeig, said he: – he said rather otherwise, that if he sailed into Breidafirth he would visit your homestead and choose a wife from your home, and have kindling to burn your steading if he so wished. The same if he sailed into Borgarfirth, for he had heard that it was no long path from the sea up to Borg, and if he sailed into Eyjafirth he would visit Jarnskeggi's farm. In the same way if he sailed into the East Firths he might happen on Skegg-Broddi's house. Now, it is no matter to him if he never returns to Iceland, and you will get what you deserve from this, and that is shame and disgrace. Yet it seems poor to me, such a good chieftain as you have been, that your lot should be so scant, and I would spare you that.

Gellir answers: – This must be true; and I would care little if there were some tricky way around the confiscation. I let friends lead me into it rather than set my own mind on it.

Ofeig spoke: – Once your big hurry has slowed down you will see that the worthier part is to marry your daughter to my son Odd, as I said at first. See the money here that he sends you, and with it the word that he would himself provide her dowry, knowing that you are hard up; and these two hundred of silver are hardly to be matched. Think, now, who offers you such a choice, to marry your daughter to a man who himself provides her dowry, yourself never like to be short of money, and your daughter come into plenty?

Gellir answers: – That is so much that it is hard to comprehend. Yet nothing will bring me to betray those who trust me, though I see nothing come of the suit but scorn and derision.

Ofeig answers: – Wonderful minds you have, you chieftains. Who has urged you to betray those who trusted you, or to go back on your oath? On the contrary, it may happen that the award will come under your decision, and you can then lessen the sum and yet hold to your oath.

Gellir said: – That is true, and you are a very crafty old fellow, and wonderfully shrewd, and yet I cannot contend alone with all the rest of them.

Ofeig spoke: – How if I bring in another, will you then help with the plan?

That I will, said Gellir, if you order it so that I have a say in the award.

Ofeig spoke: – Which one do you choose to be with you?

Gellir answers: – Egil is my choice, he lives nearest me.

Ofeig answers: – Unheard of! Choose the one who is worst of your lot! It is too much to ask that I honour him thus, and I do not know that I will go so far.

You decide, then, said Gellir.

Ofeig spoke: – Will you take part if I bring him in with you? For he will surely see which is better, to have some honour, or none.

Since I stand to gain so much, said Gellir, I think I shall risk it.

Then Ofeig said: – Egil and I have already had some talk, and he thinks it a not unduly difficult plan, and he has come in. Now I shall give some advice as to how it should go. You Schemers and your men mostly move about together; no-one will be suspicious if you and Egil get talking together on the way to evensong as the notion takes you.

Gellir accepts the money, and this is now agreed between them. Ofeig moves off towards Egil's booth, and neither slow nor this way and that way, and not bowed over. He tells Egil how things stand. He is well pleased about it. Afterwards, in the evening, men go to evensong, and Egil and Gellir have their talk and put this together between them. No-one suspects what they are up to.

CHAPTER 10: It is said that next day men go to the Law Rock, and there was a crowd. Egil and Gellir gather their friends with them. Ofeig was in Styrmir and Thorarin's company. And when those expected were at the Law Rock, Ofeig called for silence and spoke: —

I have taken no part in my son Odd's case before now, though it was begun with an irregularity hitherto unheard of, and so followed up and likely to end so, and yet I know that men are here now who have been most pressing for it. The first I shall address is Hermund. I shall ask whether or not a settlement will be accepted.

Hermund answers: — We shall accept nothing but self-judgement.

Ofeig spoke: — That one man should grant self-judgement to eight in a single case has hardly been known, though there are precedents for one granting it to one. However, since this has gone forward already with greater irregularity than any such ever before, I shall allow that two may act for your party.

Hermund answers: — We shall agree to this to be sure, and care not which two act.

Then you will grant me the trifling privilege, said

Ofeig, of choosing the two that I wish from among you Schemers?

Ay, said Hermund. Ay.

Then Thorarin spoke: — Only ay today what you will not regret tomorrow.

I shall not take back my words now, said Hermund.

Ofeig seeks men as sureties, and they were easily found, because the money seemed securely placed. They take hands and shake hands on the payment of whatever sum is fixed as settlement by the men Ofeig names, and the Schemers then shake hands on the dropping of the suit. Now it is intended that they shall go up on the fields with their men. Gellir and Egil's men keep together. All sit in one place in a ring, and Ofeig goes into the ring, peers about and lifts the hood of his cloak, strokes his arms and stands somewhat straighter, with his shoulders thrown back, flickers his eyes and spoke: —

There you sit, Styrmir, and all will wonder if I do not elect you in a case that concerns me, for I am one of your thing men, and must look to you for support, and you have had many good gifts from me, and all ill rewarded. As I see it, you were first of this lot to show enmity to my son Odd, and most responsible for having the charge taken up, and I choose you out.

There you sit, Thorarin, said Ofeig, and truly, no-one will maintain that you do not have the wit to judge here, and yet you have needlessly helped to put Odd in this fork, and you were first man with Styrmir to give your support to the Scheme, and for this I choose you out.

There you sit, Hermund, mighty chieftain, and I do not doubt that the case would be in good hands if it were to come into yours, and yet no man has been so dead set as you since the beginning, and you have shown that you wish to be seen as dishonourable. Nothing has brought you into it, what is more, but mere shamelessness and greed, for you are not hard up for money, and I choose you out.

There you sit, Jarnskeggi, and you think yourself quite up to the matter, and you would not take it ill if it did come under you. And your self-esteem rose to such heights that you had a banner carried before you at the Vodla Thing, the way they carry them before kings. Now I do not know how high your self-esteem may not mount up if honour comes your way from this, and I choose you out.

Now Ofeig looks about, and he spoke: – There you sit, Skegg-Broddi, and is it true that when you were with him King Harald Sigurdsson said he thought you fittest of the men here in Iceland to be king?

Broddi answered: – The King often spoke well of me, but it is not certain that he meant all he said.

Then Ofeig spoke: – You shall king it over something else, and I choose you out.

There you sit, Gellir, said Ofeig, and nothing has brought you into this but sheer avarice, and yet you have this excuse, that you are hard up for money and have much to take care of. Now I do not know but I think you all deserve the worst, yet someone must have the dignity of handling the case, and because few are left, and I am in no mind to choose those whom I have already chosen out, I take you because you have not heretofore been known for injustice.

There you sit, Thorgeir Halldoruson, says Ofeig, and it is clear that no case amounting to anything has come under you because you do not know how to weigh such things; and have no more wit for it than an ox or an ass, and I choose you out.

Then Ofeig looks about, and a verse came to his lips.

Ill bide all men
age's onset;
reason and sight
rives she from all;
mine was the pick
of worthy men,
wolf's tail only
waits now on the hook.

And I have fared as the wolves: they eat right on and come to the tail before they know. I have had to choose among many chieftains, and now only that one is left who will seem a bad choice to everyone, and truly he is the most high-handed of the lot and does not care how money is made so long as he gets more; and yet there is this excuse for his unscrupulousness that many have entangled themselves in the Scheme who have heretofore been thought right-minded, and have given up their honesty and goodness and become greedy rascals. Now, it will enter no-one's head that I may choose a man everyone expects to be wicked, for there is not a craftier to be found in your lot, and yet that is what it must come down to, since the rest are already chosen out.

Egil spoke, and with a grin: — Once again, as many a time before, no honour comes my way because others want me to have it; and the time is at hand, Gellir, up we stand and go somewhere and talk the thing over between us.

And so they do, off they go elsewhere and sit themselves down.

Then Gellir spoke: — What shall we make it, then?

Egil spoke: — Here is what I propose, that we set a small fine; and I do not know what else may come of it, but there will be little friendliness for our share.

Will it not be quite enough if we make it thirteen ounces of no-good money, said Gellir, because the case was undertaken very wrongfully, and the less they like it the better. But I am not eager to declare the terms of the settlement, for I expect them to be ill received.

Do which you like, said Egil: make the declaration or take on the answering.

Then I choose, said Gellir, to declare the terms.

Now they go to face the Schemers.

Then Hermund spoke: — Up we stand, then, and hear tell of our shamelessness.

Then Gellir spoke: — Time will not make us wiser, and it will all come out the same, and the settlement Egil and I have made is to award us Schemers thirteen ounces of silver.

Then Hermund says: — Do I understand right, did you say thirteen times ten ounces of silver?

Egil answers: — It was not so, Hermund, that you were sitting on your good ear before you stood up. Thirteen ounces it is, and those of bits that no-one worth anything would take. They will be paid in shield scraps and fragments of arm rings, and all the poorest stuff that can be had and you will like least.

Then Hermund spoke: — You have cheated us now, Egil.

Have I so? says Egil. Do you think yourself cheated?

Cheated I do think myself, and you have cheated me.

Egil answers: — I am well satisfied to cheat him who trusts no-one, and not himself either, and I can find proofs for what I say about that. You hid your money in such a thick fog that you meant to keep it hidden from yourself too, in case you took the notion to hunt for it.

Hermund answers: — This is like that other lie you told, Egil, what you said last winter when you got back home to that empty larder of a farm I had invited you from for Yule, and you were glad I did, as might be expected. And when Yule was over you turned glum, as might be expected, and thought poorly of going back to hunger, and when I saw that, I invited you to stay on, and one other of your folk with you, and you accepted and cheered up. And then in springtime, after Easter, when you got home to Borg, you said that thirty of my wintered-out horses had died on me, and all had been eaten.

Egil answers: — I do not think your stinginess can be exaggerated, but I would say that we ate either few of them or none. Everyone knows that for me and my folk there is never lack of food, though my means are far from easy, but life in your household is little to brag about.

If I have my way, says Hermund, we shall not both be at the Thing next summer.

I shall say, says Egil, what I thought I never should say, that now you open your mouth to some purpose, for it was foretold me that I should die of old age, and the sooner the trolls take you, the better I shall be pleased.

Then Styrmir spoke up: — He speaks truest of you, Egil, who speaks worst, and calls you fox.

Now it is going well, says Egil; the more you slander me, and the more proofs you find for it, the better I like it, because I was told that when you were pairing men at the drinking game, you paired yourself with me. There is no doubt, says Egil, that you have some bad faults that other men do not know about, and you must know best about yourself. And yet this is unalike between us, that each promises support to others, and I give what I can and spare nothing, but you run as soon as blackhandled axes are lifted. It is true, too, that my larder is often lean, and yet no-one goes hungry who comes to me, but you are stingy with food, and a sign of it is that you have a bowl you call Foodful, and of all who come within your fence, none knows what is in it, but only you. Now it is right enough for me that my household should live hard when there is nothing for them, but not so fitting, for those who have plenty, to let their households go hungry, and you know who they may be!

Styrmir holds his peace.

Then Thorarin stands up.

Egil spoke: – Quiet you, Thorarin, and sit down and do not put in a word! There are tales I can tell about you that for your sake were better not told. And I do not think it laughable, though the boys laugh at it, that you sit with your knees squeezed up and rub your thighs together.

Thorarin answers: – Take good advice wherever it comes from.

Sits down and holds his peace.

Then Thorgeir spoke: – Everyone can see that this is a paltry and foolish settlement, to award thirteen ounces of silver and not more in such an important suit.

But I expected that you would see this as a notable award, said Egil, and so you will if you think about it, for you must remember the Rang River Leet, when a certain cotter marked your head with thirteen bumps, and you took thirteen ewes with lamb in compensation, and I meant that you should be glad of this reminder.

Thorgeir held his peace, and Skegg-Broddi and Jarnskeggi desired no bandying of words with Egil.

Then Ofeig said: – Now I shall speak a verse for you, and to many it will be a reminder of this Thing, and the conclusion to which this lawsuit has been brought: –

> More praise, less meriting,
> men ask, than I bask in;
> come dwarfs' mead and call my
> keen wit to words fitting.
> Wise hatlands, I wound them
> wool-flannel-bound, truly;
> blew sand to make blear-eyed
> big doers, did this poor one.

Egil answers: – You may well brag of this, that never has one man more thoroughly sailed upwind of so many chieftains.

After this men walk back to their booths.

Then Gellir spoke to Egil: – My proposal is that we keep together with our men.

They do so.

There are strong enmities in what remains of the Thing, and the schemers were much dissatisfied with the outcome of their case. And this silver, not one of them will have it, and it gets strewn about on the fields there. Now men ride home from the Thing.

CHAPTER 11: Now father and son meet, and Odd was

ship-shape for sea. Then Ofeig tells Odd that he has given them self-judgement.

Odd answers: – Bad work, to leave the case like that!

Ofeig answers: – All is not lost yet, kinsman.

He gives a full account of how it went, and says that a wife has been promised him. Odd thanks him for his support, and thinks he has followed it through far beyond what he thought possible, and assures him that he will henceforth never be short of money.

Now you must sail, said Ofeig, as you have purposed, and your marriage will be at Mel six weeks before winter.

After this father and son part lovingly, and Odd puts to sea and is given a good wind north to Thorgeirsfirth, and merchants are already harbouring there. Then the good wind dropped, and they lie up some nights. Odd thinks the wind is slow coming, and he climbs a high fell and sees that there is a different wind out at sea, comes back to his knarr and says that they are to row on out of the firth. The Norwegians scoff at them and say it will be a long row to Norway.

Odd says: – Who knows? Perhaps you will be waiting here when we come back.

No sooner are they out of the firth than they pick up a favourable wind and do not lower their sail before they are in Orkney. Odd buys malt and grain there, stays a while and readies his ship, and when he is ready an east wind comes and they set sail. Fair weather all the way, and they arrive at Thorgeirsfirth, and the merchants were still there. Odd sails west around the coast and arrives in Midfirth. He had been away seven weeks.

A feast is now made ready for which there is no lack, everything needed for such is in great plenty. A crowd comes too; Gellir and Egil came and many other important men, and it is an occasion of magnificence. Men thought they had taken part in no finer wedding here in Iceland. And when the feasting is over, guests were seen on their way with rich gifts, and most money was laid out when it came to Gellir's part.

Then Gellir spoke to Odd: — I wish that Egil might be well done by, for he is deserving of it.

It seems to me, said Odd, that my father has done well by him already.

Make it better, though, says Gellir.

Gellir rides away now, and his folk.

Egil rides away, and Odd sees him off and thanks him for his help: — and I shall not do as well by you as I ought, but yesterday I let herd sixty wethers and two oxen south to Borg; they will be waiting at home for you, and you shall not be in want as long as we both are living.

Now they part, and Egil is mightily pleased, and they confirm their friendship. Egil rides home to Borg.

CHAPTER 12: That same fall Hermund gathers men and rides out to Hvamm's Leet, meaning to carry on to Borg and burn Egil in. And when they come out by Valfell they hear as it were a bowstring twang up on the fell, and next thing Hermund feels that he is ill, and there is a sharp pain under his arm, they have to turn back in their ride, and his illness grows worse. And when they arrive by Thorgautsstadir he must be lifted from his horse. The priest is sent for from Sidumuli, and when he gets there Hermund could not speak, and the priest was there beside him. And once when the priest leans over him there comes from his lips: — Two hundred in the gully, two hundred in the gully.

Then he dies, and so his life came to its end, as is told here now.

Odd lives on his estate in great magnificence, and in much love with his wife.

All this while nothing is heard of Ospak.

The man, Mar, took over Svala, and he was the son of Hildir, and he moved into the farm at Svalastadir. His brother was Bjalfi, a simpleton, and very strong.

There was a man Bergthor who lived at Bodvarsholar. He had summed up the case when Ospak was made outlaw. It happened one evening at Bodvarsholar, when folk were sitting by the fires, that a man came and knocked at the door and bade the farmer come out. The farmer becomes aware that it is Ospak and said he would not go out. Ospak urges him much but he goes out none the more for that and forbids his folk to go out, and such was the parting between them. And in the morning, when the women came into the byre, nine cows had been killed. This became widely known.

And again, after a while has passed, it happens that a man goes to Svalastadir and into the building where Mar sleeps; it was early in the morning. He goes to the bed and stabs Mar with a sax so that it goes straightway into his guts. The man was Ospak. He spoke a verse: —

> Drew from its sheath
> New-sharpened blade;
> into Mar deep
> let drive did I;
> heir of Hildir,
> him I grant not
> bliss of Svala's
> bedded embrace.

And when he turns to the door Bjalfi leaps up and stabs him with a whittling knife. Ospak walks to the farm that is called Borgarhol and there publishes the killing. Then he goes away, and nothing is heard of him for a while.

The killing of Mar became widely known and was ill spoken of. Then came the news that the best stud Odd owned, five horses, were all found dead, and the deed was attributed to Ospak. Now there is a long while when nothing is heard of him. And in the fall, when the men went after the wethers, they found a cave among some crags, and in it a man dead, and by him stood a basin full of blood, and that was black as tar. The man was Ospak, and it was thought that the stab Bjalfi gave him would have hurt him so that he perished at last for want of care; and so ended his life. It is not told that there was a case at law over the killing of Mar or the killing of Ospak.

Odd lives on at Mel to old age and is thought a very notable man. The men of Midfirth are descended from him, Snorri Kalfsson and many other mighty men. From this time forth the friendship and kinship between father and son held well. And there this story ends.

End-notes

CHAPTER 1: **Twelve ells of homespun**: the Icelandic word for homespun was *vaðmál*, which means 'measured cloth', *vað* being cognate with archaic English 'weed' (clothing), and *mál* with 'measure', as in the second element of English 'piecemeal'. *Vaðmál* was for long a medium of exchange in Scandinavia, before livestock and fish partly took its place, and, to some degree, gold and silver. In Iceland *vaðmál* continued to be woven on the upright loom long after this had been displaced elsewhere by the horizontal loom. It was a woollen cloth, usually felted, and dyed with natural dyes, and it had many uses, for clothing and bedding and also sails, caulking of boats, tenting of booths, wall hangings and other such. It was valued in early years at six ells to one ounce of silver, but had decreased in value to forty-eight ells to the ounce of silver at approximately the time that Odd took his from the wall. It came to be a considerable export from Iceland, and its quality was then regulated (cf. Dennis, Foote and Perkins, pp. 36–37, 12).

CHAPTER 2: **Odd's purchase of a new chieftaincy**. It seems likely that this was meant to be the *Melmannagoðorð*, one of three established when Iceland was divided into quarters. Before this there had been thirty-six chieftains; now there were thirty-nine. At the same time, or approximately, nine more chieftaincies were established whose duties were limited to the Althing. The term 'new chieftaincy' seems to apply specifically to the three that were added in the north quarter at the time of the administrative division. Along with the thirty-six 'full and ancient' chieftaincies these three assumed the duties of hallowing the spring and post-Althing assemblies. Odd shows his ignorance of the law both in his handing over of his chieftaincy to Ospak and his claiming it back; these should have taken place at an assembly and in the presence of witnesses (cf. Dennis, Foote and Perkins, K 84, p. 136; Magerøy, note to 4/28–30, p. 41; and Guðni Jónsson, p. 301, n.1).

CHAPTER 4: **Ospak's courtship of Svala** and her acceptance are both very casual. The M text of the saga, from which the translation was made, does not speak of marriage. The other old text, known as K, does, but the M version is probably true to the original on this point (cf. Magerøy, xliv ff. and note 7/9–10, p. 43). If Svala was younger than twenty, which seems likely enough, her 'betrothal' (*fastna* is the Icelandic verb) was unlawful, and so it would have been in any case without a marriage ceremony and some approval of kin. The superficiality of her nature is revealed in her attachment to Mar soon after Ospak has been outlawed. The Icelandic says that Mar took her to wife (*Sá maðr fekk Svölu er Már hét*).

Summoning days. Odd rode with twenty men to summon Ospak for thievery, a charge he would have to answer, or have answered for him, at the Althing. The summoning would be lawfully performed, four weeks before the Althing in the hearing of the prescribed number of men. Vali talks Odd into waiting till he makes one last effort towards reconciliation, and then takes the death blow from Ospak that was intended for Odd. Ospak's regret for this killing adds a touch that gives depth to his portrayal as a villain. Vali's death, at the same time, makes him a sacrifice, a suggestion of Baldr in his characterization.

Summonings were fraught with risk, and in this one the stage was set for a killing, of Odd or Ospak or perhaps both. But that was not how the story was to go. Ospak then made the event more charged with seriousness by vanishing without having published the killing and so making himself at once guilty of *mord*, and therefore an outlaw, without recourse, to be hunted down and killed and his property confiscated. But the story drops him at this point and does not take him up again till the end, after the flyting at the Althing and Odd's marriage have both been acted out.

CHAPTER 5: **Odd 'treads us and our thing men all under foot'**. Guðni Jónsson (*IF* VII, p 318, n.1) suggests that the bitterness in this observation may be that of a holder of one of the 'full and ancient chieftaincies' against a newcomer who has bought himself one of the newly-instituted ones.

Odd says nothing and ponders his words ... Odd's legal ignorance is important to the plot, which has been contrived to place Ofeig at center stage. Odd had arranged for the members of his panel to be present at the Thing, but it was there that he should actually summon them to appear in court. If a member was absent he should appoint a substitute at the Thing itself. There seems to have been no regulation providing specifically for a member who dies, but this must have been accepted as analogous (cf. Magerøy, n. to 11/12–14, p. 47).

Ofeig takes over. It is an ironic touch that Ofeig is one of Styrmir's thing-men. Ofeig's second appearance in the story is as sharp-tongued as his first, but more dramatic, coming as it does immediately after the first check Odd has received in the self-assurance of his play. Ofeig is in a black cloak, which is to say that it is of dyed cloth and is therefore, initially at least, a garment of some value, and his staff has been made with a point. He is an ambiguous figure, he may be comical but there is a suggestion of *Óðinn* in his peering glance and his get-up. The sympathetic side of his character soon comes to the surface. And he is in command of this scene, as he is of the rest of the saga, till Odd takes over again early in Chapter 11.

CHAPTER 10: **Hermund's wintered-out horses:** soon after the conversion to Christianity the eating of horse meat, which had been an important food at pagan sacrificial festivities, was forbidden by the Church. It was a common, coarse reproach at this time to accuse a man of eating horse meat (cf. Magerøy, note to 31/20–21, p. 59).

Bibliographical References

1. Magerøy: *Bandamanna saga*, ed. Hallvard Magerøy. Viking Society for Northern Research, University College London, and Dreyers Forlag, Oslo. 1981. The text on which the present translation is based. Glossary by Peter Foote. Notes englished by Peter Foote and Sue Margeson.

2. Dennis, Foote and Perkins: *Laws of Early Iceland, Grágás 1*, translated and supplied with Introduction, glossaries and a Guide to Technical Vocabulary by Andrew Dennis, Peter Foote and Richard Perkins. University of Manitoba Press, Winnipeg, 1980. (An especially valuable reference for *The Saga of the Schemers*.)

3. Guðni Jónsson: *Íslenzk Fornrit VII*, ed Guðni Jónsson. Reykjavík, 1936.

Víga-Glúm

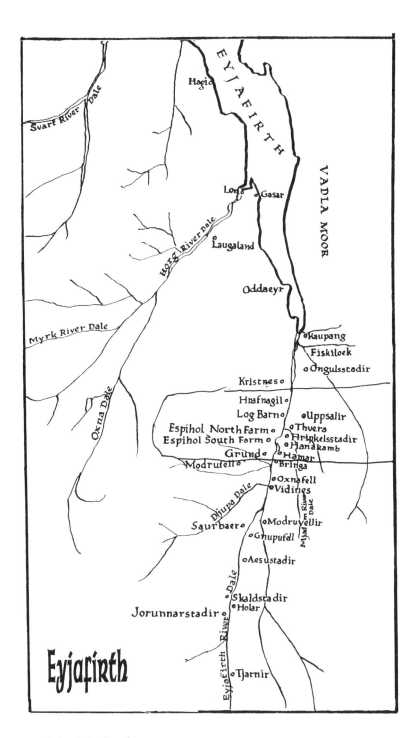

Eyjafirth

'Map B', detail – see page 7.

Eyjafirth

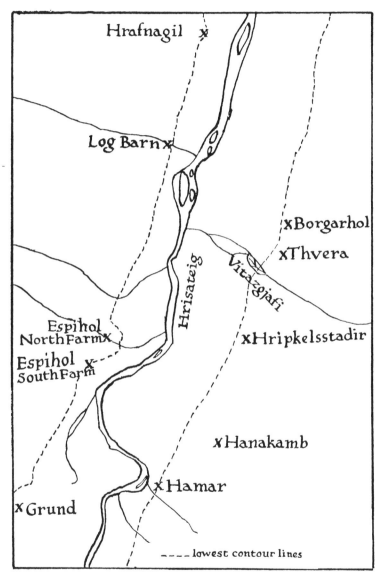

'Map B', detail – see page 7.

CHAPTER 1: There was a man Ingjald, son of Helgi the lean; he lived at Thvera in Eyjafirth. He had one of the full and ancient chieftaincies, and was a mighty chieftain and a very old man when this story took place. He was a married man and had two sons, Steinolf and Eyjolf. They were men of many accomplishments, and both handsome. Ingjald was self-willed and taciturn, quarrelsome and headstrong. He had little love for merchants, wanted none of their arrogance towards him. If he desired something from them he sent other men for it and did not go himself.

A ship came into Eyjafirth one summer; Hreidar was the skipper, a man of noble stock. He had a farm at Voss in Norway; a most valiant man and well-liked. Eyjolf Ingjaldsson was often at the ship during the summer and he and Hreidar shared a warm friendship. Hreidar said to him that he would overwinter here, and would most prefer to be with Ingjald, from what he had heard of him. Eyjolf says his father has not made that his custom but agrees that he will do what he can about it. When he comes home he puts it to his father that he should take in the skipper, whom he considers to be an honourable man and most worthy, and he made a good case for the skipper to him.

Ingjald answers: – If you have already invited him, what need is there to say more? It will be for me to bear the cost, then, and you shall have the work it will take: – said he had never had an outlander stay with him before and would still as soon not.

Then Eyjolf says: – Nothing has been done yet without your consent; but so it is that I have little to say about what goes on, nor do you intend that I shall have much, if a man I have asked is not to be given his keep here.

Ingjald answers: — Then you shall arrange as you will for the captain to come here with one other man. I shall not impose on him for your sake, and you shall do all the work for them and I shall see to the cost.

He answers: — I am glad to have it so.

Next day he goes and meets Hreidar and tells him how it is. He shows his pleasure, and he and his goods are moved in. Before long Hreidar became aware that there was to be a Yule feast with many guests. Ingjald spoke little with him, but he was civil.

One day Hreidar asks Ingjald to the outbuilding where his goods were kept, and he comes. Hreidar spoke then and bade him choose what he will among the goods. Ingjald said he did not desire his goods, but he calls his offer manly.

Hreidar answers: — Yet I have given some thought to what you should receive from us. I have been in some houses that are among the best in Eyjafirth, and I have seen no such rooms as here. But your wall-hangings are not so fine that their like is not to be found in other houses.

He took wall-hangings from his stores and gave them to Ingjald, and they are very fine, none finer had come here to Iceland before. Ingjald thanked him warmly, and now there was great friendliness between them.

Then during the winter Eyjolf says to Hreidar that he wants to go east to Norway with him in the spring. He was not quick to answer.

Eyjolf says: — Will you not take me? Do you not like me much?

Very much, says he, but your father will think he has had a poor return for my keep here, and I shall not repay him so ill as to take his son abroad who is such a source of pride to him. But if your father were to allow it, I should gladly take you and be most grateful to have you.

Now the merchants made ready for their voyage, and when they were ready Eyjolf again spoke to Hreidar about sailing east with him.

He told him his mind, said he did not want to cross his father over this of his sailing east.

Then Eyjolf tells his father of his eagerness to travel, and what had passed between Hreidar and him.

Ingjald says that few men would be so worthy as Hreidar: – and since you ask well, and I have had experience of his worth, I shall grant you the voyage, and think it better that you go with him than with another.

CHAPTER 2: They sailed east, then, and arrived in Norway. Hreidar made many suggestions as to where Eyjolf might find his keep, but he would not fall in with what he proposed.

Hreidar spoke: – What do you wish to do then?

He answers: – I do not know.

Then Hreidar says: – Are you not keen to visit kings or other chieftains. You have a right to our help. Service with chieftains would seem good for you powerful men who are likely to be staunch followers.

Hakon Athelstan's foster-son was king of Norway then.

Eyjolf answers: – I am not up to service with kings, though perhaps I should like it well enough; nevertheless I say no to that.

Hreidar asks: – What do you want to do then?

Why do you back off asking me to stay with you, when that is what I wish?

I have little mind to do that, says Hreidar.

Eyjolf asks: – Why should that be?

I should not wish to offer what it would not be good for you to accept, for I think you deserve nothing but good from me.

I am curious to know why that should be.

You must be told, then, though it ill becomes me to tell it. I have a brother whose name is Ivar. We own the farm and all our goods together and we love each other dearly, but we are not of the same mind in this way, that he thinks poorly of Icelanders, so that there is no life for them with us. He is away raiding every summer, and when he comes home he brings nine or eleven men with him to our place, and all at hand must wait on them, and they will be so ugly with you that you will never put up with it.

Eyjolf answers: – I am curious to see how they behave, and you are blameless if you are providing hospitality.

Hreidar answers: – I owe it to my brother, who brings the best gifts he can find and gives them to me, not to break with him over you; and yet I shall take it badly if they make sport of you and jeer at you.

You do wish to avoid having me come with you, says Eyjolf, but how will he be with me? He will not strike at me, will he?

Hreidar answers: – It will be worse than a beating. He has many bad men with him. They will twist everything you say or do to your face.

Eyjolf says: – There is nothing hard about that if a man knows it is coming; it would be foolish not to put up with such things, nor will that stand in the way.

Hreidar says: – There is trouble in it on either hand:

you are my friend and he is my brother, and I love him dearly.

It came about, that he went to lodge with Hreidar in Voss. When Ivar was expected, Eyjolf got a frieze cloak and wore it every day. He was a big man, and always sat next to Hreidar.

CHAPTER 3: Now Ivar comes home, and he is met with due honour and warm greetings. The brothers each asked the other's news, and where Hreidar had been over the winter; he said he had been in Iceland. Then Ivar asked for no more news: — but what is there beside you, he said, man or beast? That is no small lump.

Eyjolf answers: — I am an Icelander, I am called Eyjolf, and I shall be here for the winter.

My guess is, said Ivar, that the farm will not be without trouble if an Icelander is to be here.

Hreidar answers: — If you are so ugly with him that he cannot put up with it, the bond of our kinship will suffer.

It was an unlucky voyage that you made to Iceland if we are to serve Icelanders on account of it, or be estranged from kinsmen or friends. I do not know why you think it good to go there among that worst kind of folk, and now you need tell none of your news to me.

Quite the contrary, declared Hreidar; many honourable men live there.

Ivar says: — This is not right, though, having this hairy lump in a high seat.

But when Ivar saw that his brother set great store by this man he has less to say against Icelanders than before: — but what other can I do than call him Lump?

Eyjolf said that the name would do very well; yet whatever he said or did, they twisted it.

There was a man Vigfus; he was a chieftain and ruled in Voss. He was son of Sigurd, son of Viking-Kari; he had a daughter Astrid. There was close friendship between the brothers and Vigfus; they feasted each other at Yule by turns, and this year it was for the brothers to give the feast. Hreidar had made all ready and should now invite the guests, and he bade Eyjolf come with him: – for I have no wish to know how they will behave with you.

I am not well, says Eyjolf, and therefore I cannot come.

That evening when Hreidar had gone and they were on the benches, Ivar's fellows said: – Lump is at home and Hreidar is not; now we shall have what sport we like.

What we shall rather do now, says Ivar, is think what befits us. Here we are two brothers and have everything in common, and he has all the care of it and I none, and this is a man he wants to have as his guest, and the way we go on his life is hardly bearable, yet he has done nothing to us, and no man is to say anything ugly about him while Hreidar is not at home.

They say that the time is right to be having some sport.

Then Ivar spoke: – There is little manliness in your talk: everyone waits on us here and we make sport of everything as we please, while others have the work and care. And supposing this man had killed a brother of mine, yet for Hreidar's sake I should do him no harm. I shall not put up with any making fun of him, and no-one is to call him Lump any longer.

In the morning Ivar spoke to Eyjolf: — Will you come to the forest with us and pass the time?

He agrees and goes with them; and they cut timber to bring home. Eyjolf has a sword and hand-axe.

Ivar spoke: — I advise you, Icelander, if we go our separate ways, that you come home before dark.

They all made off their different ways in the forest, and Eyjolf went by himself. He took off his cloak and laid his sword, which he had been holding in his hand, on top of it. He went about in the forest enjoying the time, and he had his axe and cut timber that looked right to him. As the day wore on it began to snow. He then thinks of making for home, and he came to where the cloak had been lying. It was gone, but the sword was left behind. He sees that the snow has been swept as though the cloak had been dragged over it. A wood-bear had come and dragged the cloak away; its strength had been barely enough to hold it up, for it was a young bear and had just come out of its den, and not killed anyone. He went on and saw that the bear was lying in wait for him; swung his sword and cut the snout from the beast up by the eyes, and had that in his hand as he was coming home.

Ivar got home first and, missing Eyjolf, he spoke: — It was not right for us to go on, we did badly in parting from our mate. He does not know the forest and the likelihood of many wild beasts in it. There will be heavy talk if he does not come home, the way we have been towards him, and I say we search for him till we find him.

But as they came out before the doorway, Eyjolf walked towards them. Ivar greeted him gladly and asked why he was bloody, and he showed them what he had in his hand.

Then Ivar spoke: — I am afraid that you are hurt. Be easy about that, nothing has hurt me.

Then Ivar spoke: — It is a fool's game to make fun of men we do not know; he has shown courage where I think none of us would have ventured.

Next evening Hreidar came home.

Ivar spoke: — Why are you so silent, brother? Are you anxious about Lump? What do you think now? How have I treated him?

Hreidar answers: — How you have done that will indeed matter between us.

He says: — What will you give then, to have me be with him as you are?

He answers: — I shall give you the gold ring that we own together and you have always thought good.

He says: — I do not covet what your father left you. I shall treat him henceforth as I do you, and he shall sit next to me and not next to you.

Thereafter they both made much of him, and acknowledged that a good man occupied the place he sat in. And so it went thenceforward.

CHAPTER 4: Men come now to the brothers' Yule feast. Benches were set in order for pair-drinking, and lots drawn for who should sit next to Astrid, daughter of Vigfus the chieftain, and Eyjolf always drew to sit beside her, though no-one saw them talking together more than with others. Yet many did say that it must have happened so because she was the woman fated for him.

The feasting came to an end, and it had been nobly provided, and the men seen on their ways with gifts.

Eyjolf was four summers on viking raids, and was

thought a most bold and fearless man; he won fame and much wealth.

One winter the man whose name was Thorstein came to Voss; he was a kinsman of the brothers and had a farm in Upplond. He told of the strait he was in, that the berserk named Asgaut had challenged him to a duel on account of his having denied him his sister, and he asked them to stand by him with their numbers at the duel, so that this viking should gain no foothold on what was his. He said that Asgaut had killed many of his men, moreover, and he would lose his sister if they would not lend him their strength: – I lack confidence for the duel unless I have your luck with me to face him.

They would not refuse to go with him.

They ride to Upplond with him and had thirty men, and they come to the place where the meeting is to be. Then they put it to their men: who among them would win the woman for himself by going in and duelling with Asgaut?

But though the woman seemed a prize, no-one was ready to fight for her.

Then the brothers asked Eyjolf if he would hold the shield before Thorstein.

Eyjolf says that he has not done that for any man, and not for himself: – and I would think poorly of it if he were killed on my hands, I see no honour in that. And if this young man is killed on our hands, shall we ride home with such an outcome, or shall we put up another and then a third, and our shame increase as more fall, to our loss? Our coming will have been worth little if we go back and leave it unavenged that he has fallen, to our loss. Ask me rather to duel with the berserk; that is what is owing to a friend, but the other I will not do.

They thank him much; yet it seemed a heavy commitment on his part.

He says: – It seems to me that there will be no returning home for any of us if he is not avenged, and I would think it worse to fight the berserk after your kinsman had already been killed.

With this he goes in, and Ivar offered to hold the shield before him.

Eyjolf answers: – That is well offered, but this most concerns me, and the old saying holds, that *Self's hand is surest*.

He goes on to the duelling ground then.

The berserk spoke: – Is this big brute to fight with me?

Eyjolf spoke: – You are not afraid to fight with me, are you? Perhaps you do not know better than to tremble before a big man and swagger before small ones.

No-one has said that about me, says he, but I shall repeat the law to you as it bears on duelling: three marks will buy me off the duel if I am wounded.

Eyjolf answers: – I shall not be bound by law with you when you are judge of your worth, because in our land what you have set for yourself would be called slave's wergild.

It was for Eyjolf to strike first, and his stroke hit the tail of the shield, and off went the tail and the berserk's leg too. Eyjolf achieved much fame by this deed, and he went home with the brothers afterwards. He was now offered a great sum of money, but he said that he had not done this for money nor to win the woman, but rather out of friendship for the brothers. Asgaut bought himself off from the duel and lived on, a cripple.

Then Eyjolf asked for the hand of Astrid Vigfus's daughter. Ivar and Hreidar are there to put forward his suit; they say he is of noble stock and has high standing in Iceland and strong support of kinsmen. They said he had great prospects.

Then Eyjolf spoke: — It may be that our suit seems presumptuous to Astrid's kinsmen, but many in Iceland know that we have noble forebears and great riches.

Vigfus says: — This must be her destiny, though we had intended nothing less distinguished for our daughter.

She was married to him, and went out to Iceland with him.

CHAPTER 5: There was a man Bodvar; he was son of Viking-Kari and brother of Sigurd, father of Vigfus; Bodvar was father of Astrid, mother of Eirik, father of Astrid, mother of Olaf Tryggvason. Viking-Kari was son of Eymund field-spoiler, son of Thorir. Bodvar was the father of Olof, mother of Gizur the white.

When Eyjolf returned to Iceland with Astrid, Ingjald was dead. Then Eyjolf took over the farm and chieftainship. Ulfeid was Ingjald's daughter; Hrisey-Narfi was married to her. Eyjolf and Astrid's four children are named. Thorstein was their eldest son; he was given his portion of the family wealth when he married, and he dwelt at Holar in Eyjafirth while he lived. He takes little part in the story. Vigfus was the second; he married Hallfrid, daughter of Thorkel the tall of Myvatn. Glúm was their youngest son, and Helga their daughter. She was married to Steingrim of Sigluvik. Their son was Thorvald tasaldi, who comes into the story later. Vigfus died soon after he married; he had one child that not long outlived him, and then all the remaining family wealth, after Thorstein's portion, was equally divided, one portion in the hands of Hallfrid and Thorkel the tall, the other with Astrid, for Eyjolf was dead when the story comes to this point. †

Thorkel the tall moved to Thvera with Sigmund his son. Sigmund was a bold and ambitious man, and meant to acquire a chieftainship if he married well and his wife's kin stood by him.

There was a man Thorir; he lived at Espihol. He was son of Hamund darkskin and Ingunn, daughter of Helgi the lean. He was married to Thordis, Kadal's daughter. Their children were Thorarin and Thorvald hook, who lived at Grund in Eyjafirth, and Thorgrim, who lived at Modruvellir, and Ingunn, whose husband was Thord, priest of Frey, and Vigdis, who became Sigmund Thorkelsson's wife.

Thorkel and Sigmund took to making things hård for Astrid. The land had been divided between Thorkel and Astrid, as has been told, and Astrid and her son Glúm

---

† Both genealogies are important. The first makes the connection between Gizur the white, Teitsson, and the famous Norwegian king, Olaf Tryggvason. Gizur's two appearances in the story are brief but important: first in Chapter 9, when he supports Glúm in his victorious case at law, and again, in Chapter 25, at the fateful oath-swearing, after which Glúm gives him the blue cloak Vigfus had passed on to him. Another man named Gizur appears in the genealogy in Chapter 10. His part in the story is significant but brief, and it is entirely told in Chapters 10 and 11. The second genealogy introduces the main characters involved in Glúm's triumph at law in Chapter 9, which establishes his career.

got the half that had no building. They set up house at Borgarhol. Glúm did not exert himself in the running of the farm; he seemed a backward one in his early years. He spoke seldom and then said little. He was a tall man, with somewhat slanting eyebrows, fair-haired and straight-haired; a spindly and seemingly slow-witted man; did not go to gatherings. Astrid and Glúm's wealth begins to dwindle and their affairs come into a bad state. Thorkel and Sigmund bear in on them, and they get the worst of everything.

There was a temple to Frey south of the river at Hripkelsstadir.

Thorarin, son of Thorir of Espihol, was a wise and well-liked man. His brother, Thorvald hook, was a dueller, and quarrelsome. Sigmund Thorkelsson thought himself a mighty man when he married into kinship with these Espihol men.

Glúm tells his mother that he wants to go away east:
— I see that my manhood will come to nothing here, and it may be that I shall get luck from my noble kinfolk. I have no mind to put up with Sigmund's push, though I see that I am not the one to confront him yet. But do not let any of the land go, however pressed your lot may be.

Glúm was fifteen years old when he would go away east.

CHAPTER 6: Now to tell of Glúm's voyage from Iceland. As soon as he arrived in Norway he went up to Vigfus, at Voss. And when he got to the farm he saw a crowd of people, and many kinds of sport and play; it seemed to him that everything had a look of magnificence. But where he saw many noteworthy men he could not tell which might be Vigfus, his kinsman. He had this mark of him, that he saw a man who was tall and of noble bearing in the high seat, wearing a dark blue hooded cloak, and he was playing with a gold-inlaid spear. He went to him and greeted him, and his greeting was well received.

Vigfus asked him what kind of man he would be, and he said he was an Icelander, and of Eyjafirth.

Then Vigfus asked about Eyjolf, his son-in-law, and Astrid, his daughter, and he replied that he was dead: – but Astrid is living.

Vigfus asked who of their children were living, and Glúm told him of his brother and sister. Then he told him that one of their sons was now before him, and when he said that the talk broke off. Glúm asked to be shown where his seat was to be, and Vigfus said that he did not know what truth there might be in what he had told him. He pointed to a place for him on the outer bench by the door, and showed him little respect.

Glúm had little to say, and kept to himself. While other men were drinking and enjoying themselves in many ways, he lay with his cloak over his head, and seemed simply a fool.

A winter-night feast was made ready, and a sacrifice to the disir; all were to take part in these rites. Glúm stays in his place and does not go to them. As the evening went on and guests had come, the jollity was not what might have been expected, such cheer and meeting of friends as there was, and so many gathered there. That day, when folk had come to the feast, Glúm had not gone out to meet them, nor had he asked anyone to sit by him, or in his place, and when they were seated at table it was said that the man Bjorn, called ironskull, had come to the farm with eleven men. He was a mighty berserk. It was his way to seek large gatherings and talk with them, and perhaps one would say something he could take up, and challenge him to a duel about it. Vigfus told them they should choose their words carefully: − for there is less indignity in that than taking more trouble from him. They promised him, readily.

Bjorn walked into the hall and looked for men to greet him. He asked the outermost man on the higher-rank bench if he was as valorous as himself and the man replied: − far from it! Then he asked one after the other till he came to the high seat. They found different answers, but all meant the same, that none was his equal in valour. When he came to Vigfus he asked him where he might expect to find such a champion, and Vigfus acknowledged that he did not know Bjorn's equal. Then Bjorn spoke: − Well answered and wisely, as would be expected. You are a most worthy man, and your life has been long and as you would wish it, and no decline in your fame and honour. Now, it is well that I need only have good words with you, but I shall ask if you consider yourself my equal.

He answers: − When I was young and out raiding and won some glory I do not know but I might match myself with you; now, however, far less, when I am old and worn out.

Bjorn turns away then and goes outwards along the other bench and again asks if they think they are as valorous as he; and they agreed that they were not so valorous. Then he came to where Glúm was lying on the raised floor.

Why does this man lie so, said Bjorn, and not sit up?

His benchmates answered and spoke up for him and said that he was so witless that no heed need be taken of what he might say.

Bjorn spurned at him with his foot and said he should sit up like other men, and asked if he would be as doughty as him.

Glúm said he need not have to do with him, and said he knew nothing about his doughtiness: – I shall not compare myself with you at all because out in Iceland a man would be called fool who took on the way you do. But here I find everyone humble in what he says.

With that Glúm jumps up at him, wrenches the helmet from his head, snatches up a firebrand and brings it down between his shoulders. The champion buckles under this. Then another blow and another, till he fell. He tried to get to his feet but Glúm hit him on the head and kept at it till he got out through the door.

When Glúm turned to go back to his place, Vigfus and all the others had stepped out on the floor, and now Vigfus greeted his kinsman warmly; said he had given proof that he was of his stock: – I shall honour you now, as befits us both. Said he had behaved otherwise at first because he thought him unpromising: – I should wait till you proved your lineage by your manliness.

He leads him to a seat beside his own. Glúm said he would accept that seat, and indeed would have done so sooner.

Next day they are told of Bjorn's death. Vigfus invited Glúm to take over his authority after him, and his chieftaincy, and Glúm says he will accept this, but go out to Iceland first, so that those whom he begrudged the use of his patrimony should not encroach on it; said he would come back at his first opportunity.

Vigfus said he thought it would be Glúm's destiny to enlarge their family and fame in Iceland.

In summer Vigfus has a ship got ready for Glúm and gives him cargo for it and much treasure in gold and silver, and he spoke: – My heart tells me that we shall not see each other again. Here are special gifts I would give you: this cloak and spear and sword that we have put much trust in, we kinsmen. As long as you keep these gifts I foresee that you will not lose your worthy standing, but I am fearful of that if you let them out of your hands.

Then they part.

CHAPTER 7: Now Glúm sails out to Iceland and home to Thvera. He went to his mother straightway and she welcomed him gladly and told him of the injustice of Thorkel and his son; bade him be patient towards them, however, and said she was little able to take action against them. After this he rode out as far as the garth wall. He saw that the wall had been moved and bore in on his share; then he spoke a verse:

> Bear in on the borders,
> bold ones, of my holdings:
> green walls I begrudge their
> greed. Let them heed, woman.
> Injure my ancestral
> acres, who mistake me:
> sword leaps from my scabbard
> swift, as my heart lifts it.

And this had been going on out here in Iceland meanwhile: Sigmund had been making things hard for

Astrid, and would drive her from her farmstead. In the fall, while Glúm had been abroad, two heifers went missing that belonged to Thorkel and Sigmund, and they thought they had been stolen, most likely by slaves that Astrid owned. They say that the slaves have eaten them in secret, and summoned them in the spring for theft. And these slaves were most faithful overseers and workmen for Astrid. She thought she could hardly keep up the farm if they were not there. She goes to see Thorstein her son and tells him what harm Thorkel and Sigmund are doing her, and asks him to answer for the slaves: — I will rather pay money for them than let them be sentenced on a false charge if there is no better answer for it. It seems to me that you ought to stand shield for us now, and show that you are of good stock.

Thorstein said he thought that the case would be put forward by them in such a way that they would mean it to have the support of their kinsmen by marriage: — It seems wise to me, if your housekeeping is dependent on these men, that I have some part in settling it by paying compensation.

She answers: — I know in my heart that the only compensation will be one that is meant to do us harm, and since little help is to be expected from you, the decision is bound to be left to them.

Certain great benefits came with Thveraland. They came with the grain field that was called Vitazgjafi, for it was never barren. It had been so allotted in dividing the property that each had the use of it in alternate summers, Astrid one summer and Thorkel the next.

Astrid now says to Thorkel and his son: — I can see that you would do me and my household much harm, knowing that a strong hand is lacking here. But rather than let the slaves be given up I am willing to put the case to your judgement.

They called this the wiser course, and decide what they will do. Their decision was to have self-judgement in the matter of the slaves, or outlaw them. Thorstein backed the case so feebly that Thorkel and Sigmund got self-judgement, and they awarded themselves the grain field, that they alone should own it. They meant to acquire the land altogether by taking away the prop that had been the chief support of Astrid's housekeeping. That very summer she should have had the use of the grain field if it had gone by rights. During the summer, however, when men had ridden to the Thing where this case was settled, a herdsman went round the pastures and found the heifers in a landslide, and they had been snowed under at the beginning of winter. Now the falseness of the accusation against the slaves came to light.

When Thorkel and his son heard that the heifers had been found they offered money to pay for the field but would not give up their right to it.

Astrid says it would not be too much to make up for the slander if she got back her own: − and I shall either have what is properly mine or do without. Though no-one wants to set the case to rights now, I shall wait, and I expect that Glúm will come back and do that for us.

Sigmund says: − He will be slow to put his hand to the plough, when the likelier of your sons sits idly by.

She says: − Pride often comes to a bad fall, Sigmund, and injustice too. That may well apply to you.

A little later in the summer Glúm arrived in Iceland, and he does not stay long with the ship; rides home with much wealth. His temper was as before, he had little to say and made as though he had not heard what had been going on here meanwhile. Every day he slept till mid morning and did not exert himself about the farm.

That summer Glúm and his mother should have had the grain field if all had gone by rights. Sigmund's cattle did much damage to their place and were in their home field every morning. One morning Astrid woke Glúm and said that Sigmund's herd had come into the home field and would break up the haycocks: − I am not spry enough to drive them away, and the men are off at their work.

He answers: − Seldom have you called me to work, and I shall not take it ill that you do so now.

He springs out of bed, catches his horse, takes a cudgel in hand and drives the cattle briskly; thumps them hard till they run into Thorkel and Sigmund's home field; leaves them there to do what harm they will.

Thorkel saw to the hay harvest at home in the mornings and Sigmund went with the hands. Thorkel spoke to Glúm: − You can be sure that men will not put up with your hurting their cattle, though you think you have made a name for yourself abroad.

Glúm told him his cattle were all unharmed now: − but if they come and trouble us again they will not be left all unbattered, and you may content yourself with that; that is all you can do; we shall not put up with more trouble from your cattle.

Then Thorkel spoke: − You are bragging now, Glúm, but you seem the same fool to us as you did when you went away east, and we shall not run our affairs according to your brag.

Glúm turned for home, and laughing broke out in him; he was so moved that he turned pale in the face, and from his eyes there fell such tears that they were like, as it were, hailstones that are big. He was often so moved later, when the killing mood was in him.

CHAPTER 8 : The story tells that when autumn was setting in, Astrid came and spoke to Glúm again one morning and woke him and told him to get the work organized; said that the hay crop would be got in today if it were gone about as it should be. Sigmund and his father had got their hay in a while since: – and Sigmund and Vigdis went out early this morning to Vitazgjafi, and they must be glad that they have the field which we should be having if things went by rights.

Then Glúm got up, but was not ready, however, before mid-morning. He put on the dark blue cloak and took the gold inlaid spear in his hand; let saddle his horse.

And Astrid said: – You choose most carefully how you dress for the haying, my son.

Glúm said: – It is not often that I go to work, and I shall get much done and be fittingly clothed for it too, and yet I do not know well how to go about the work. I shall ride up to Holar and take his offer to stay there from Thorstein my brother.

Then he rode southwards over the river. And when he came to the field he took the pin from his cloak. Vigdis and Sigmund were in the field, and when Vigdis saw him she came towards him and bade him welcome: – it seems poor to us that there is so little feeling of kinship between us. We wish in every way that there might be more.

Glúm answers: – Nothing has happened yet that all may not be well about our kinship. I have turned this way, however, because the pin has come from my cloak, and I wish you might sew the fastening on.

She said she would do that willingly, and she did.

Glúm looked over the field and spoke: – Vitazgjafi again has not failed us.

He put on his cloak and took his spear in hand. Then he turns towards Sigmund and brandished the spear. Sigmund sprang up to face him, Glúm straightway struck him in the head, and Sigmund needed no more.

Then he went to Vigdis and said that she should go home: – and say to Thorkel that Sigmund cannot leave the field on his own.

Glúm rode up to Holar and told his brother no news. But when Thorstein saw how he was clothed and armed, that he had both cloak and spear, then he saw the blood in the gold work and asks if he had struck a blow with it not long since.

He answers: – That is so; it did not come into my mind to tell you, said Glúm. I killed Sigmund Thorkelsson today.

Thorstein says: – That will seem news to Thorkel, and to the Espihol men too, his kin by marriage.

Glúm answers: – It is an old saying that Briskest are men on a blood night. They will cease to make much of it as time passes.

Glúm was there three nights on his visit, then he readies for home. Thorstein offers to go with him. Glúm says there is no need for that: – take care of your farm; I shall ride my straight road to Thvera. They will not stir themselves much to follow this up.

Glúm rides home to Thvera.

And when these tidings were told, Thorkel went to meet Thorarin, and asks advice from him as to how he should proceed.

Thorarin says: – It may be that Astrid says now that not for nothing has he got up on his leg.

Thorkel says: – I think he has got up on the leg that he will not make walk for him.

Thorarin answers: – That is now to be seen. You have been behaving unjustly towards them a long while, and you have meant to push them to the wall and hardly gave a thought to what might be expected from the son of such a man as Eyjolf was, a man from mighty stock and a very tough fighter as well. And we are much bound to Glúm on kinship's account, and to you on account of marriage. It looks a difficult case to me if Glúm presses it, as I would guess will happen.

Thorkel rode home and this matter lay quiet over the winter. Glúm then had a few more men on hand than was usual for him.

CHAPTER 9: The story tells that Glúm had a dream one night; he dreamed that he was standing outside his home and looking towards the firth. He dreamed he saw a woman walking inland across the district, and she made from there towards Thvera; and she was so big that her shoulders touched the mountains on either side. He dreamed that he went out of the garth towards her and called her to him; then he woke up.

It seemed strange to them all, but he says this: – The dream is much and full of meaning. Here is how I read it, that Vigfus my mother's father must now be dead, and this woman who walked higher than the hills must be his fetch. He was in the forefront beyond other men in most kinds of worthiness, and his fetch will be seeking her homestead here, where I am.

In the summer, when ships came west to Iceland, they heard of the death of Vigfus. Then Glúm spoke a verse: —

> Hugely, head-dress goddess
> helm-crowned, fell-surrounded,
> firthward saw I faring
> forth, adornment goddess.
> Dreamed I warfare's dreadful
> deity, slain men's greeter,
> stood by fells, of stately
> stature, tree of battle.

In the spring Thorkel met with Thorvald hook and other sons of Thorir to seek their support in following up this case. He spoke of obligation to their sister, Vigdis, his daughter by marriage, and of many friendly things he had done for them as well, he and Sigmund, his son. Thorvald meets Thorarin, says that shame will come on them unless they follow up the case of their brother-in-law, says he wants to put everything in his power behind it: — and it is easy to see now that Glúm means to make much of himself by the killing of Sigmund, but we take ourselves to be of no lower standing in the district.

Thorarin says: — I see a difficulty that goes with this case, there is no certainty that we shall improve our standing by it. Moreover we shall be contending with Glúm's luck. He will most likely take after his kin and ancestors. Therefore I move less confidently in this than you, for honour seems dubious to me in a contention with Glúm. I think it not good either if we come into greater dishonour.

Nevertheless, after more urging, Thorarin Thorisson prepared the case against Glúm for the killing of Sigmund. Glúm prepared the case against Thorkel the tall on account of the false accusation against the slaves, and he prepared another against Sigmund, and summoned him for theft, declared that he was on his land when he killed him, and he summons him as one without sanctity before the law because he had fallen on his land. He dug Sigmund up to do so. Then the case went forward to the Althing on that footing, and Glúm sought the support of his kinsmen, Gizur the white and Teit the son of Ketilbjorn from Mosfell, and Asgrim Ellida-Grimsson. He tells them the whole story, the bullying of Thorkel and his son and their injustice and their many insults. He said he expected support towards a just settlement from their side but would himself be in charge. They said they were all under obligation that his lot should not lie in unfriendly hands and declared they would be glad of a rise in his standing for the good of their family.

The Thing moves on to the court hearings, and the Espihol men bring forward the charge of manslaughter, rather on the urging of those who had injuries to remember than in any confidence that it would be without flaws. Glúm puts the case against Thorkel, and the suits come into the court: he had much support of kinsmen and friends. When the defence was called he says: — As matters stand, many must know that you have rather made your case on wrong grounds than without flaws, for it was on my land that I killed Sigmund, and before I rode to the Thing I summoned him as one unsanctified according to the law.

He named witnesses and in this manner defended the case, and his kinsmen stood by his claim that Sigmund fell unsanctified according to the law.

Then Glúm puts forward the case against Thorkel for his fraudulent attempts on his property, and it looks unhopeful for Thorkel because witnesses came forward for Glúm, and against these no defence was found. It seemed likely that Thorkel would be convicted. A settlement was sought with Glúm. He says there are two choices, that he should press the case to a judgement, or else Thorkel should sell him Thveraland at the price he would name, and that was not more than half its worth: – and let Thorkel think of this, that if he is convicted we shall not both be at the Thing next summer.

Now Thorkel's friends put in their word that he should settle, and Thorkel took that course, as behoved him, accepted the terms and sold Glúm the land. He should stay on it that year, and there was what might be called a settlement, and the Espihol men were ill content with the outcome. And henceforth there was never a healing between Glúm and the Espihol men.

Before Thorkel moved away from Thvera he went to Frey's temple and led an old ox there and spoke thus: – Frey, said he, you have long been my trusted one; you have had many gifts at my hand and repaid them well. I give you my ox for this, that Glúm may go no readier of heart from Thveraland than I do now. And let me be given a sign as to whether you accept it or not.

The ox made answer thus, that he bellowed and fell down dead; and Thorkel thought it a good sign, and he was now in better heart, for it seemed to him that his petition had been received. He moved north to Myvatn then and lived there, and he is out of the story.

CHAPTER 10: Glúm now acquired great standing in the district.

The man lived at Lon in Horgardal who was called Gunnstein, a mighty man and rich, counted among the great ones. He had married the woman who was called Hlif. Their son was Thorgrim who was known by his mother's name and called Hlifsson because she lived longer than Gunnstein; she was a woman of note. Thorgrim was gifted in the manly arts and he became a great man. Grim was another of their sons, he was called bankleg. Halldora was their daughter; she was a beautiful woman and fine natured. As a match she was thought one of the best, for her family's sake, and yet most for her skills and strength of character. Glúm asked for this woman; said there was little need for his kinsmen to tell of his family or of his wealth either, or how he lived: – these must be known to you, and I have meant this match for myself provided her kinsmen are willing.

He was given a good answer to this asking; she is betrothed to Glúm with much wealth, and their wedding is a fine one. And now his state is yet worthier than before.

There was a man Thorvald Refsson who lived at Bard in Fljot; he was married to Thurid, daughter of Thord of Hofdi. Their children were Klaufi, and Thorgerd whom Thorarin of Espihol married. Thorvald hook of Grund was married to Thorkatla of Thjorsardal. Hlenni the old, son of Ornolf bagback, lived at Vidiness, and he was married to Oddkatla, daughter of Oddkel of Thjorsardal.

There was a man Gizur Kadalsson. He lived at Tjarnir in Eyjafjardardal. He was married to the woman Saldis, a full good housewife. Gizur was also counted among the greater farmers, very rich. Of their daughters two are named, Thordis and Herthrud, beautiful women and very showy; they were thought to be good matches; they grew up at home. The brother of Gizur was Runolf; he was father of Valgerd, mother of Eyjolf of Modruvellir. Thordis was Kadal's daughter who was married to Thorir of Espihol; their children were told of before. Thorgrim Thorisson was not Thordis' son, though born in wedlock.

Thorgrim, son of Thorir of Espihol, was a great man and accomplished. He rides to see Gizur with this purpose, to ask for Thordis his daughter to be his wife. The pleaders for the proposal were his brothers and friends, kinsmen of the woman; they thought of themselves as having a rightful say about the marriage of their kinswoman, and thought it most promisingly asked for. But Thorgrim was denied the woman. To all it seemed that he had asked for an even match, and his brothers and kinsmen were offended.

CHAPTER 11: The man Arnor is named into the story, called redcheek. He was the son of Steinolf Ingjaldsson, and cousin to Glúm on his father's side. He had long been a sea trader and was well thought of, and he was always with Glúm when he was in Iceland. He put it to Glúm that he ask the hand of a woman for him. Glúm asks what woman he is to speak for.

Arnor says: — Thordis Gizur's daughter, who was refused to Thorgrim Thorisson.

Glúm says: — I think that looks unpromising, for I can

see no difference between you two. But Thorgrim has a good farmstead and much property, much support of kinsmen, and you have no farm and not enough wealth. And I do not want to press Gizur unfairly, so that he does not decide for his daughter the way he would wish, for he deserves well of me.

Arnor says: — I benefit by good kin if I make a better match because you put forward my case. Promise him your friendship and he will give the woman, for this would have been thought an even match if a goodly man like Thorgrim had not been refused before.

Glúm let himself be persuaded. He went with him to see Gizur and put the proposal to him.

Gizur answers: — Glúm, says he, it may be said that my judgement is failing if I give my daughter to Arnor, your cousin, and did not see my way to letting Thorgrim have her.

Glúm says: — Truly spoken, and yet it should be made clear that if you honour our suit my friendship comes in return.

Gizur answers: — That seems worth much to me, and yet I suspect that enmity to match it will come from other men.

Glúm says: — You shall make up your mind yourself, yet my attitude will be much affected by what you decide.

Then Gizur says: — You will not depart empty-handed this time.

He reached out his hand, and Arnor is betrothed to the woman.

Glúm says that for his part the wedding shall be at Thverª in the fall. They leave now, with this understanding.

Arnor had malt out at Gasar and he was to go after it himself and one farm hand with him. Thorgrim Thorisson went that day to the hot springs when they were expected from the coast with the malt, and was at the Hrafnagil springs, and six of his hands with him. When Arnor and his man came from the coast and would ride across the river, Thorgrim spoke: – Does it not fall out very well that we meet Arnor and his man? We shall not lose the malt though we lose the woman.

Thorgrim and his men walked up towards them with drawn swords; and when Arnor and his men saw how unequal their numbers were they plunged into the water and so across the river, and the pack-horses were west of the river.

Then Thorgrim spoke: – We are not unlucky in everything; we shall drink the ale and they will have the say about the woman.

Thorgrim rides to the Espihol south farm. Thorir was then blind.

Thorgrim's company were in high spirits and laughed much, and Thorir asks what they found so laughable. They said they did not know who first would hold the feast; said the supplies were with them and the owners chased away: – and the bridegroom got a ducking.

When Thorir hears this he spoke: – You think your prank a good one when you laugh so much, but what way out is there for you now? Do you mean to sleep here tonight and nothing else needed? You do not know Glúm's temper if you expect him to think well of his kinsman's journey. I call it wise to gather men; most likely Glúm has already gathered many men.

There was a ford in the river then where there is none now. They gathered eighty fighting men during the night and stationed themselves on the end of the ridge, because the ford in the river was right by it.

And it is to be told of Arnor that he goes to Glúm and tells him how he has fared.

He says: — It comes as no surprise to me that they have not let it lie quiet, and now if it stays quiet there is trouble enough — disgrace, and no certainty of honour if an attempt is made to put it right. Nevertheless we shall now get men together.

At first light next morning Glúm came up to the river with sixty men, and made to ride across. The Espihol men hurled stones at them, and that ride did not take place. Glúm turned back and they fought across the river with stones and missiles, and many were hurt there, but no-one is named.

When the men of the district became aware of the strife they thronged there during the day and came between them. A truce was struck and the question put, what would the Espihol men offer for the insult they had given Arnor? Back came the answer that no payment would be forthcoming for Arnor's running away from his malt packs. Then it was proposed that Glúm should take part in asking the hand of Herthrud, another of Gizur's daughters, for Thorgrim, and then only should the marriage of Arnor and Thordis take place if Glúm won this woman for Thorgrim, and she was thought to be making the better match whom Thorgrim married.

Now, since many put in their word, Glúm promises his endeavour, meets Gizur and opens this proposal, and he said: — It may seem meddlesome if I seek wives for my kinsmen and the men of Espihol too. But that troubles may come to an end in the district, I feel bound to grant you my loyal support if you do as I wish.

Gizur answers: – What you suggest seems best to me, for I should think my daughter well married this way.

Both sides now accept this solution. A little later Gizur died. Then Saldis moved her dwelling to Uppsalir. Arnor got a son by Thordis who was called Steinolf. Thorgrim also had a son and he was called Arngrim, and his childhood was altogether most promising.

CHAPTER 12: Saldis invited her daughters' sons to live with her, the two of them. Arngrim was two years older than Steinolf, and no better-liked lads grew up in Eyjafirth, or more accomplished in every way, and they loved each other dearly. When one was four years old and the other six they were playing together one day, and Steinolf asked Arngrim to lend him his tin horse.

Arngrim answered: – I shall give it to you because it is now rather your toy than mine, at our ages.

And Steinolf told his grandmother how fine a gift he had received. She said it was well done, that they were so good to each other.

The woman used to go about the district whose name was Oddbjorg, a merry heart, wise and foreknowing. It seemed important that the housewives give her a good welcome. Her words were more or less favourable according to how she was entertained. She came to Uppsalir and Saldis gave her a good welcome and bade her foretell something about the boys, foretell something good.

She says: – These lads show promise if their luck holds, but to me that is not clear.

Saldis spoke: – I think you do not much like what I give you, when you make such a scoff.

She answers: — What you feed me has no bearing; there is no call to be so touchy.

Saldis spoke: — Keep it to yourself if you can think of nothing good to say.

She says: — I have hardly said much about it yet, but I do not see a lasting affection between them.

Saldis spoke: — I thought my good hospitality deserved something better, and you will be driven away if you foretell ill.

Oddbjorg says: — I think there is no need to hold back now since you carry on so, for no cause; nor shall I come to your place again, and you may like that as you will; and this I can tell you, it is with killing spears that they will later fight each other, and one worse thing after another will come of that, here in the district.

Now Oddbjorg is out of the story.

CHAPTER 13: It happened one summer at the Althing that the Northerners and Westfirthers took up sides on the wrestling slope; it went worse for the Northerners; at their head was Mar, son of Glúm. A man came up to him whose name was Ingolf Thorvaldsson. His father lived in the Rang River plains.

Mar spoke: — You are a sturdy looking man; you must be strong. Come and wrestle for us.

He answers: — I shall do that for your sake.

Down went the first who came against him; a second came and a third and the same happened. The Northerners now plucked up heart.

Then Mar spoke: — If you need my support I shall be for you, but what are your plans?

He answers: — I have planned nothing, and I want most to go north and find work.

Mar says: — I wish that you would come with me, and I shall find you lodging.

Ingolf had a fine stud of horses, and he called the stallion Snaekol. He went north from the Thing to Thvera; was there a while.

One day Mar asked Ingolf what he meant to do: — we have need of a manager here and he should have some skill. Here is a sledge which you shall mend, and you are a skilled man if you know how to do that.

Ingolf answers: — I should like to stay here most, but it has happened sometimes that my horses have been thought harmful in the stock pasture.

Mar says: — Nothing will be made of such a thing here.

Ingolf then repairs the sledge, and Glúm comes and looks at his carpentry.

That is well done, says Glúm, but what are your plans, then?

Ingolf answers: — I have not made plans.

Glúm says: — I need a manager, but are you able that way at all?

He answers: — Hardly for such a place as this, and yet I should be keen to stay with you.

Glúm says: — Why should you not? I can see that you and Mar have become friends.

Then Mar comes home and Ingolf tells him.

He answers: — That seems good to me if it goes well. I shall tell you three times if my father becomes displeased, and if you do nothing about it I shall say no more.

Ingolf then takes on the management and Glúm is well pleased.

One day Glúm goes to a horse fight with his

manager; the manager rides a mare and his stallion runs alongside. The sport there is good. Kalf from Log Barn farm was there. He had an old jade, and it got the better of every horse.

He spoke: — Why should that precious beast of the Thvera men not be brought against him?

Glúm answers: — That is no match, the stallion and your jade.

He says: — You must be holding back because there is no heart in him then; perhaps the old saying is true, Like master, like beast.

Glúm answers: — You would know nothing about that, and I shall not say no for him, but it is to last no longer than he chooses.

Kalf says: — It is to be expected that little happens against your will.

The horses were brought together and fought well, and it seemed to everyone that Ingolf's horse had the better of it, and Glúm will then part them. They ride home. Ingolf is there that year and Glúm is well pleased with him.

There was a gathering at Djupadal River. Glúm comes to it with Ingolf and his stallion. Kalf comes; he was a friend of the men of Espihol. His stallion was with him and he proposes that they now take this horse fight to a finish. Glúm says that Ingolf shall decide. He acknowledged that he was not keen, but did not want to back out. The horses are brought together; Kalf whips his horse; Ingolf's horse has the better of it in every round. Then Kalf strikes Ingolf's horse close by the ear so that he is stunned and then immediately brought his horse to the attack. Glúm goes up then and the fighting is made fair again, and it ends with Kalf's horse going out of the ring. Then a great shout went up. And when they parted, Kalf struck Ingolf with his stick. Now men stand between them.

Glúm spoke: – Give no heed to such things, it ends this way here at every horse meeting.

Mar spoke with Ingolf: – My father means you to take no dishonour from this blow.

CHAPTER 14: There was a man Thorkel who lived at Hamar. Ingolf goes there and meets with the daughter of the farmer; she was a handsome woman. Her father was well off. He was not an important man. Ingolf keeps up his management well at home, but does less carpentry than before.

Mar spoke to him about it once: – I see now that my father dislikes your being away from the house.

Ingolf makes a good answer and yet goes back to his same way. Mar speaks to him a second time and then a third but to no effect.

It was one evening when he came home late and they had eaten, that Glúm spoke: – Now we shall choose patrons and have some pastime; I shall choose first and my patrons are three: one is my purse, second my axe, third storehouse.

Then one after the other chose.

Then Glúm spoke: – What do you choose, Ingolf?

He answers: – Thorkel of Hamar.

Glúm springs up and holds his sword hilt before him and went at him and spoke: – A fitting patron you choose for yourself.

All saw that Glúm was angry. He went out and Ingolf with him.

Then Glúm spoke with Ingolf: – Go to your patron

now and say that you have killed Barn-Kalf.

He answers: – Why am I to lie about myself?

You are to do as I will.

They walked on together, and Glúm turns aside into the barn and saw a calf there and strikes it on the head and gives him the sword all bloody: – go south now across the river and say to your patron that only there can you expect shelter, and show him the bloody sword, that the token may be clear.

He does so, meets Thorkel and told him what had happened, that he remembered the blow Kalf had given him, and said he had killed him: – and I ask the shelter here that you have spoken about.

He answers: – You are a great fool, killed a good man, and out you go as quick as you know how; I do not intend to have you killed in my house.

He goes home and meets Glúm and he asks: – How did he prove, your patron?

Ingolf answers: – He did not prove well.

Glúm says: – Now prove my patronage, then.

He goes with him into an outside storehouse: – you will be in trouble if that Barn-Kalf has been killed.

Next day comes the news that Barn-Kalf of Log Barn has been killed. And now Thorkel says that the man who acknowledged this bad deed had come to his place. All take this to be true.

The winter passes. Glúm sends Ingolf north to Einar Konalsson and gives him a thousand ells of homespun, and spoke: – You have had no wages from me, but with your sense for trade you can turn this to your profit. I shall take over the charge that is brought against you and you will not suffer; I paid you that for your stubborness. And if you come back out you may visit me.

Ingolf spoke: — I ask that you do not let the woman be married away from me.

This I promise you.

His horses stayed behind.

Einar Konalsson got Ingolf abroad. Thorvald readied a case over the killing of Kalf for Hegraness Thing, and it looked as though Ingolf would be outlawed. Glúm was there too and some of Ingolf's kinsmen. They meet Glúm and ask for his help and tell him that among them they are willing to make up compensation for him.

Glúm answers: — I shall see this case through with no compensation paid.

When the courts went out to sit and a defence was called, Glúm said that the case was void: — you have charged another man than the one who did the killing, and I am guilty of the killing. Then he names witnesses that the case is void: — and though Ingolf did kill a barn calf I brought no charge against him for that. Now I shall offer a settlement more in accord with what the man was worth than with the arrogance of you Espihol men.

Men rode home from the Thing.

Ingolf was abroad that winter and was content to stay no longer; trades his goods and buys fine things and wall-hangings that were rich pieces. Glúm had given him a good cloak; he traded that for a tunic of fine cloth.

That summer when he had gone east, the man came out to Iceland whose name was Thjodolf. His mother lived at Aesustadir. He rides to Hamar and meets with Helga. One day Glúm had ridden up to Holar, and as he was riding down to Saurbaer, Thjodolf rode along towards him.

Then Glúm said: — I do not like your visiting at

Hamar. I mean to make Helga's marriage my business, and if you do not leave off I shall challenge you to a duel.

He answers that he would not set himself against Glúm, and leaves off his visits.

CHAPTER 15: Now Ingolf comes back out to Iceland and rides to Thvera, and Glúm welcomes him and offers him lodging. He accepts this.

One day Ingolf spoke: – Now, Glúm, I would have you look over my goods.

He does so, and it seems to him that he has traded well.

Then Ingolf spoke: – You stocked me to pay my way; I call you owner of these goods.

Glúm says: – The goods are yours only, I do not intend them for mine.

Here are wall-hangings, however, that I have bought to give you, you must accept these, and here is a tunic.

Glúm answers: – I shall accept your gifts.

One day Glúm asks if Ingolf wanted to be at home with him.

Ingolf answers: – It is in my heart not to part from you if I am to choose; I shall give you my stud of horses.

Glúm says: – I shall accept the horses, and now we shall meet with Thorkel of Hamar today.

They do so. Thorkel gives Glúm a good welcome.

Then Glúm spoke: – You made a false accusation against Ingolf and you may put that right in this way, by marrying your daughter to him. He is right for this match and I shall put money into his portion. I have proved him a good man, and if you do not agree to this you will find out your mistake.

He agrees, and Ingolf marries the woman and becomes a farmer and ready-handed man.

CHAPTER 16: Glúm married his daughter Thorlaug to a man called Killing-Cavern of Myvatn in the north, but because they could not get along he let her go home to Thvera and divorced her. Glúm liked this not at all. Then Arnor hagnose asked for her and married her. From them have come distinguished men. After this there was much ill will between Glúm and Cavern.

One summer a vagabond came to see Cavern and asked to be taken in.

He asked what was his trouble.

He confessed to killings and to having no safety in his district.

Cavern says: – I do not know that I am under obligation to you, but what will you do to earn my protection?

He answers: – What are you driving at?

Cavern says: – You shall do an errand for me to Viga-Glúm, and say in these words to him that you think you need to have him take over the management of your affairs. I would expect you to meet him now on his ride to the Thing. He is good in tight corners if men need him, and it may be that he will tell you to go to Thvera and wait for him there. You shall say that you are more pressed and would rather speak with him alone, and then it may be that he will have some advice about that. You shall ask to meet him in Midardal, which leads up from the farm at Thvera, and his shieling stands in it; say that you would like to meet him there on a set day.

He agrees to this, and now it all goes forward as Cavern has planned. This trap-baiter comes back to Cavern and told him about it.

He says: — Then you have done your errand well, and you shall stay with me.

Now a while passes, and when the time comes that Glúm had agreed with the messenger for their meeting, Cavern rides from home with thirty men. He rides from the north and comes west across the Vodlar Moor to the rock ledge that is called Red Ledge. There they dismount.

Then Cavern spoke: — You are to stay here the while, and I shall ride in along the slope and see if there is something to catch.

As he gets into the dale he sees a man ride up from Thvera, big and in a green cloak, and he recognizes the rider as Glúm. Then he dismounted from his horse. He had a cloak over him, parti-coloured black and white, each side its own colour. He turned his horse into the clearing and then walks to the shieling, and Glúm had gone into the shieling. Cavern had a sword in his hand that had the name Fly, and a helmet on his head; he walks to the shieling door and knocked on the wall and then goes around the corner of the shieling. Glúm goes out and it so happened that he was empty-handed; sees no-one; turns to go around the shieling. Then Cavern comes between him and the shieling door. Glúm sees who he is and backs away, and the river gully was near the shieling. Cavern tells him to wait. Glúm says it would be an even match if they were evenly armed for it. He backs off towards the gully and Cavern follows after him. Glúm leaps down over the gully and Cavern finds a way where he can walk down and sees in the gully that a cloak is flapping and runs at it and immediately thrusts into it. Then he hears a voice overhead: – Little honour in spoiling men's clothes.

Cavern looks up and there he can see Glúm.

He had known about a grassy ledge under where he had jumped down.

Then Cavern spoke: – Remember this, Glúm, that you have run now and not waited for Cavern.

Glúm says: – That is true, and I wish you a no shorter run before the sun sets this evening.

Then Glúm spoke this: –

> Every shrub worth silver,
> south growing, I vouch for.
> Woodlands wolves have hidden
> well, from fell pursuers.

With this they part briefly. Glúm rides home and gathers a troop and tells them what kind of snare had been laid for him, says he would pay it back quickly. Within a short while he gathers sixty men. They ride up into the dale. Cavern went back to his horse when he and Glúm parted and rode along the slope and then he sees the mounted troop and knows that it will not do for him to meet them. He thinks of a plan for himself, breaks the blade from his spear and has the shaft for a stick, takes off the saddle and rides bareback, turns his cloak inside out, rides towards some sheep and shouts loudly. They come after him and ask if he has seen a man ride up over the rise, armed, a mighty man.

He says he has seen him.

They asked: – What are you called?

He answers: – I am called Many in Myvatn district and Few in Fiskilaek district.

They say: — You are jeering at us and making fun of us. He said he could not speak truer, and they part.

And as soon as they were gone he picked up his weapons and saddle gear; rode hard to his men.

Glúm's men meet him and said that they had found a man who had answered them nothing but jibes and told him what he had named himself.

Then you were short-sighted, says Glúm. That was Cavern you met and what truer could he say, for round Myvatn there are many caverns but in Eyjafirth in Fiskilaek district there is not a cavern, and we nearly had him. We shall ride after him again.

They come to the ridge and Cavern and his men are there in front of them. A narrow path leads up and it is better defending there with thirty men than attacking with sixty.

Cavern spoke: — You make much effort to chase me. Perhaps you think there is something to be avenged in your running away. You showed great daring when you jumped into the gully, you were not slow of foot then.

Glúm says: — True enough, and you knew how to be afraid when you made out that you were a shepherd of the Eyjafirthers and hid your weapons, and you broke one; I think you ran no shorter way than I did.

Whatever has happened so far, come and attack now with your twice our numbers.

Glúm answers: — I think we shall part this time; let it be judged as it may, on either side.

Cavern now rides north and Glúm rides home to Thvera.

CHAPTER 17: When Thorir died Thorarin built a farm north of Espihol and lived there.

Glúm got children by his wife. Mar was his son, who has been named; second was Vigfus. They were both promising men and much unlike. Mar was quiet and easygoing and Vigfus was a rough-mannered, overbearing man, a giant in strength, shrank from nothing. There was a man with Glúm whose name was Hallvard, his freedman and foster-father of Vigfus. He raked in money, a cheat in his dealings, not well spoken of; he made over his gains to Vigfus. He set up house at the farm that is called Tjorn, in Eyjafjardardal, and did not make himself better liked for that, for he was a great sneak thief from the common pasture. Vigfus was an active trader.

The man lived at Jorunnarstadir whose name was Halli, called Halli the white. He was the son of Thorbjorn. His mother was Vigdis; she was daughter of Audun rotten. He had fostered Einar Eyjolfsson, who had then come to live at Saurbaer. Halli was blind. He helped at all settling of disputes in the district, for he was both wise and just in judgement. His sons were Orm and Brusi skald, who lived at Torfufell, and Bard, who lived at Skaldsstadir. Bard was a rough-mannered and over-bearing man, fought better than other men, free with his tongue and abusive. He was married to Una, daughter of Oddkel of Thjorsardal.

One fall ten or twelve of Halli the white's wethers were missing from the common pasture and not to be found. When Halli met his son Bard he asked him what he thought had become of his wethers.

Bard answers: — It does not surprise me that wethers disappear when thieves live in the nearest house, now that Hallvard has come here into the district.

Halli says: — I wish you would prepare a case against

him and summon him for theft, and I would guess that Glúm will not give the twelve-man verdict in his favour if I have a charge of thievery to bring against him.

Bard answers: – It will be very hard to win a twelve-man verdict against that father and son.

CHAPTER 18: Now Bard prepares the case for it. And when Vigfus knows this he tells his father he does not like it that a charge of thievery is laid against his foster-father.

Glúm answers: – You know he is not to be trusted. The case will not be well thought of if he is let off by the verdict.

Vigfus says: – I wish the case might have been about bigger things.

Glúm answers: – It seems better to me that we pay for him, have him give up his farm and come here, than stake my honour for such a man.

Now men come to the Thing and the case comes to court, and Glúm is to give the twelve-man verdict. Vigfus became aware that he meant to give the verdict, went into the court and declared he would see that Glúm found it dearly bought if his foster-father were outlawed. As it worked out, Glúm quashed the case, gave the verdict in Hallvard's favour and suffered dishonour for it.

When a winter or two had passed after this, Halli lost a homefield boar that was so fat it could scarcely get up. Bard came along during the day and asked if the boar had been slaughtered. Halli said it had disappeared.

Bard answered: – He must have gone to look for those wethers that were stolen the other fall.

Halli says: – That is my guess, they have gone the

same way. Are you willing to summon Hallvard?

Bard answers: – I am, because Glúm will not give the verdict in his favour. Vigfus was responsible when he was let off before and now he is not here in the country.

Bard takes over and rides out to do the summoning. And when he meets Hallvard he brings the case to a swift close, cuts off his head. Then he told his father. Halli showed that he was not pleased about it and rides straight to Glúm, told him what had happened and offers him sole judgement. Glúm accepts this, fixes a small sum of money and saw to it that the boar and wethers were paid for, and this is well spoken of. But when Vigfus came back he took ill the killing of Hallvard.

Glúm says: – There is to be no breach of this settlement that has been made.

Now Bard and Vigfus had nothing to do with each other, even when they met.

Next summer a horse match was arranged in which all horses at hand in the district should fight. They should compete as from the upper district and the lower, each district to choose its man to judge which had done better, and the judgement stand that had been made by the men chosen. From the upper district Bard was chosen, and from the lower Vigfus Glúmsson. There were many horses and good sport. It was a very equal match and many horse fights at a time throughout the day. It ended that an equal number had fought well and an equal number retired, and they came to agree that it had been a draw.

Then Vigfus said he had a stallion that had not fought: – and he is the best of all that have come here today; bring one out against him.

Bard answers: – He looks vicious to us; we shall not set a horse against him and still call it a draw.

Vigfus says: – You have not got a horse then, yet you will not want it said that you have no match to put up.

You have kept to your honesty well, says Bard, but now it clouds over somewhat. It can be seen that you have done more standing by the pantry shelves and talking about cookery with your mother than going to horse fights, and that, no less, is how your beard gets its colour.

Vigfus laughed, and so did many others.

Halli's farm-hand comes home and was asked about the horse meeting.

The farm-hand answers: – It was called a draw.

Halli asked: – Were they agreed, Bard and Vigfus?

He answers: – Very well, though Bard had a word with Vigfus.

He asks: – What was that?

He tells him.

Halli spoke: – That is the stuff of trouble.

The farm-hand says: – Vigfus laughed at it.

Halli answers: – The way of that father and son is to laugh when they are in the killing mood.

Halli and his son Bard meet and Halli asks why it came over him to say such an ugly thing: – and I am afraid that it will bring very bad luck. There is one course, you must go abroad east to Norway and get building timber for yourself, and be away for three years. Otherwise you are doomed.

Bard says: – There would be nothing in it if you were not cowardly. This is what age does, makes you fearful for your sons.

Halli answers: – You may be a great champion but

you will hardly live safe in the district.

He acts on his father's advice and sails east.

Then Halli pays a vagabond to go into Skagafjord and farther west from there and say that Bard went abroad east and did not dare otherwise on account of Glúm and Vigfus for that one word: — and no-one has the courage to cross them in the district.

He did as Halli told him. This shift was meant to let Bard's kinsmen sit in peace in spite of what he had said.

Bard was abroad east one winter and came back then to his farm.

CHAPTER 19: Halli had kept Bard's farm while he was east and had timber cut in the woods in Midardal that belonged to Bard. Bard too had brought back much wood. He was sometimes at his own place, sometimes with his father. Bard says that he wants to fetch his timber.

Halli answers: — I wish you would not go by yourself, for it is not wise to trust Glúm and Vigfus.

Bard says that men would not be aware of their going.

He and a farm-hand with him went to fetch the timber and they had many horses. Una his wife had gone to Vidiness to be with Oddkatla her sister. Bard came there, and Hlenni Oddkatla's husband offered to send another man into the woods and Bard to stay behind. Hlenni thought that the wise course.

Bard said he did not need this.

The sisters saw him out to the garth wall, and when they turned back Una looked over her shoulder and fell in a swoon. When she came to her wits again her sister asked what she had seen.

I saw dead men coming to meet Bard and he must be doomed. We two shall not see each other again.

Now Bard and his man ride on, and a mist drifts over as they come into the woods. They tie up timber for dragging and hobble the horses.

That morning early the shepherd was up and doing at Thvera. It often happened that Vigfus met the shepherd and asked what news, and so he did this morning, and he spoke: – It is a wonder that you can always find the sheep in such darkness; never could I find sheep in such a dark mist.

He answers: – It was little for me to find the sheep; it was more for them to find their horses that I saw in the woods this morning, though they were standing near by them, and yet they were cheerful about it, and one of those two was in a green cloak and had a shield at his side.

Vigfus asks if he recognized the man.

He says he thinks it would be Bard: – because he owns the woods that they were in.

Vigfus spoke: – Get three of my horses.

Two Norwegians were guests there; Vigfus asked them to ride with him, and said he would ride to the hot springs.

He heads southwards from the farm through Laugardal.

Then the Norwegians spoke: – Where will you ride now?

He answers: – Ride on my errand first.

He rode well ahead of them. They rode above the farms southwards till they saw Bard come out of the woods with his draft horses.

Bard's man saw the pursuit and spoke: – They are riding hard after us, says he, these men.

What are you telling me? says Bard.

He answers: – Vigfus is one, and I wish we would ride away, for there is no disgrace now since we do not know what they want.

Bard says: – Vigfus will not attack me with two other men if you are not with me.

He answers: – I would much rather go on with the horses and you ride to Vidiness. There is nothing shameful in that since you are riding where you have business. What is more, you have no sure knowledge of what they are up to, riding after us, and Hlenni said you should not trust them.

Bard says: – You must ride on ahead and see that men know of it if my ride turns out to be slower than is likely, for it will be settled quickly between Vigfus and me if just we two fight it out. He is more honourable than to attack me with two other men. But if there are two of us and they are three, then they will make use of their advantage.

He did as Bard said, and Bard loosed his shield and got himself ready as seemed best to him. And when they met, Bard asks what their business might be. Vigfus said that they should not both come from this meeting alive. Bard says he is ready for this if just they two fight: – but there is no valour in three attacking one.

The Norwegians said they would have stayed home if they had understood the errand; said they could not join in if men did not come to Bard's help, since his companion had galloped off.

Vigfus told them to see how it went first. They two then fought a long while, and neither was wounded, but Vigfus suffered this disadvantage that he had to jump back every time before he could deliver a stroke. Bard had a sword and defended himself most skilfully, and he was not wounded. The Norwegians think it would be calamitous if Vigfus were laid low, they standing by, and men came to Bard's support. They run at Bard and kill him, and he was no longer breathing when Hlenni and his men came.

Vigfus and the two rode home. Glúm grumbled about this deed, and says that big troubles have now grown bigger in the district.

Halli rode to meet his foster-son Einar of Saurbaer and asks him to take up the case. He says it is only right that he should press the case for his kinsman and foster-brother. They ride to see Thorarin and ask for his support. Thorarin says he knows of no man that he would rather act against, and they bound their friendship with oaths, for this case and any other.

The case went to the Thing and a settlement was attempted. But the weight opposed to a settlement was such that there was no chance of it, for against it were law-wise and bold men, Modruvellir and Espihol men. The case ended thus, that the Norwegians were outlawed, and money was paid for Vigfus to go abroad, and three summers should be allowed him to find passage, and three places where he could live in any one year, and so he was made partial outlaw.† And he could not be at home on account of the sacredness of the place.‡ He was at Uppsalir long whiles. It was thought

---

† cf. the general note on Law and Government. Also Dennis, Foote and Perkins, *Laws of Early Iceland, Gragas 1,* pp. 92–95, 98, 117–18, Add. 37.
‡ i.e. on account of the temple of Frey.

that he was in other quarters of the country, and he would not go abroad in the allowed interval. Then he became full outlaw and Glúm kept him in hiding. It was not right for outlawed men to be there, Frey did not allow it near his temple.

Six winters passed then.

CHAPTER 20: Now the story takes up when the foster-brothers Arngrim and Steinolf are full grown. After Thorgrim died at Modruvellir, Arngrim moved to his farm and Steinolf with him, and the affection between them was as strong as it had best been. Arngrim married Thordis the daughter of Bjorn, sister of Arnor hagnose. Steinolf sailed on trading voyages and stayed with Arngrim while he was in Iceland.

It was one summer when he came back into Eyjafirth that Arngrim did not ask him to his place and did not speak to him, though they saw each other, and gave as his reason that Steinolf had been talking more with his wife Thordis than was seemly. It is the opinion of most men that there would be little in this or nothing. Then Glúm invited him, and for a few seasons he was with him when he was in Iceland. Their kinship was friendly. Steinolf was a very accomplished man.

One summer Glúm did not ask him to stay, said he wanted him to be at Uppsalir with his father: — and this is why I do not ask you, that I do not like this living in other people's houses. If you are with your father, then you may come here to Thvera and I shall be glad to have us meet.

Now it goes on for a few winters that Vigfus was at Uppsalir with Arnor redcheek while he was outlaw, and Steinolf was there too.

One fall a farmer in Oxnafell married off his daughter and invited all the householders of most standing in Eyjafirth. Steinolf too was invited; he came to Thvera and wanted to ride there with Glúm.

Glúm said he would not be going.

Steinolf spoke: — That seems unlikely for you.

Glúm answers: — Less harm in the unlikelihood of my behaviour than in the unwariness of yours, and I shall not go there. Big matters, says Glúm, an ordinary farmer to call in so many of the mighty ones and there be no treachery in it. I have my suspicions as to what underlies this feast. The farmer has not taken it on himself, and I think it better that my friends not go.

Steinolf went to the feast with those who had been invited, but not Glúm. There was much talk among themselves between Einar Eyjolfsson and Thorvald and Arngrim. On the day that men were to ride off Einar delivered a long harangue about the governing of the district, and said it was always fitting that many should meet together in order that what most needed saying should be said, and things would then be better: — and there has been enmity between proud-hearted men too long a while. What I am saying comes home to those kinsmen Arngrim and Steinolf. There has been hostility between them, and it is our belief that it has all come of lies and unfriendly talk. Now Arngrim would have Steinolf stay with him, and he will make his visit an honourable one if he accepts, and bury your enmity, you two.

Steinolf said he much wanted that, said he knew of no fault on his side, and said that he loved Arngrim best of men. Then everyone went home, and Steinolf went with Arngrim, and he was there for some nights and made much of.

CHAPTER 21: One day Arngrim asked Steinolf if he would like to go with him to Grund, down to the inn, and be there two nights or three.

He answers: — I shall stay home this while, and go another time when you remain here. Arngrim says it is his wish that he wait for him at home if he will not come.

Then Arngrim went to Grund and Steinolf stayed at Modruvellir for the night. And in the morning Steinolf sat by the fire and had some work in hand; it was a certain box that the housewife owned. At that moment Arngrim returned and Thorvald hook with him. And when they came into the kitchen Steinolf was bending over. Arngrim strikes him on the head so that he died immediately.

The housewife stepped up to him and spoke: — You have struck a dastard's blow; you were put up to this by cleverer men, and from this day I shall never be your wife.

She goes back to Arnor hagnose then and came never again into the same bed with Arngrim, and she said before she rode away: — You may be thankful that you have few more days of life ahead, for what you have left will get worse.

And she was later married to Asgrim Ellida-Grimsson.

Arngrim and Thorvald rode to Espihol and told Thorarin of these events and asked for his help, said they had neither wit nor men's good will to muster against Glúm. Thorarin was both wise and well-liked. He answers that the deed has an ill look and said he feared it would have an ill outcome.

Thorvald said it was no help to reproach them for the deed. He thought there would soon be more trouble for him to grapple with if he did not give them support and said they might well find more backing if he would put his word in for them.

Thorarin answers: — This is my advice, that you both move your households here from Grund and Modruvellir. Let us gather men as swiftly as we can and bring our households together before Glúm comes to know of it.

They do so before Glúm hears about it.

He gathers men as soon as he knows and goes to attack them at once, but he had missed his occasion, for the Espihol men had become too many.

They waited the winter out in quiet. Glúm was never caught off guard that winter. He was so wary about himself that he was never found in the bed that had been made for him. Often he slept little during the night, and he and Mar walked together and talked of taking legal action. One night Mar asked him how he had slept. Glúm spoke a verse: —

> Sleep comes to me slowly,
> sorely broken, warrior.
> Espihol not easily
> atones this. They know me.
> My sword will, hard swinging,
> sound on their heads, roundly;
> less has caused me loosen
> lives from mortal striving.

Now I shall tell you my dream: I dreamed I was walking here outside the garth alone and unarmed, and it seemed I saw Thorarin walking towards me, and he had a big whetstone in his hand. I seemed to be ill-prepared for our meeting. While I was thinking about it

I saw another whetstone by me and I went towards him with it. When we met, each wanted to strike the other, but the stones met, and from that came a loud clash.

Mar asks: — Would you think it might be called a household clash?

Glúm answers: — It was bigger than that.

Would you think it might be called a district clash?

Glúm answers: — That is well compared, for I seemed to know that it was heard over the whole district. And when I awoke I spoke a verse: —

> Steersman of the sturdy
> storm-elk of fjord waters
> hurled, I dreamed, and harmed my
> head with a sharp whetstone.
> Whirled I with a wielded
> whetstone too, that met him;
> so my dream wrath saw him
> served, I dreamed, worthily.

Mar said it was likely that the old saying would prove true: — Each will strike the other with an ill-meant stone, before it is over.

Glúm answers: — It is not unlikely that it will be so, much bears towards it. There is yet another dream to tell you: it seemed I was standing outdoors and I saw two women. They had a trough between them and they took their stand on Hrisateig and showered blood over the whole district. I woke up then, and I take this to be a foreboding. And he spoke a verse: —

> God-ride saw I goodly
> gleam far on these marches;

spear talk and sword whicker
show forth such high portents.
When as new blood washes
warriors, poured by valkyrs,
Odin ever gladdens,
One-eye, at men's dying.

That morning Mar went to Modruvellir with
seventeen men to summon Arngrim for the killing.
Glúm was at home with five men and bade him come
quickly back again. Jodurr was with Glúm, and Eyjolf
the son of Thorleif the tall and Thorvald tasaldi, sister's
son of Glúm, and two thralls.

CHAPTER 22: Helga, Glúm's sister, whom Steingrim of
Sigluvik married, had then moved to Laugaland. She was
mother of Thorvald tasaldi, who was eighteen years old.
    There was a man Thorvard Ornolfsson; his mother
was Yngvild, known as sister-of-all. He lived at
Kristness. Gudbrand was his son, twelve years old.
Thorvard was a clever man and was then old; he was
only middling well-intentioned. He was early afoot that
morning and told Gudbrand to fetch horses, and they
ride then to Thvera. When they got there Mar had just
ridden away.
    Glúm gives Thorvard a good welcome.
    He asks whether a settlement was being sought
between men.
    Glúm said it was not.
    Thorvard says: — Has the case been summoned?
    Glúm said it had not.
    Such a day would be right for that; fog is thick and
nobody will be aware of it if men go quietly.

Then Glúm tells him what has been done and says that six men only were at home.

Thorvard answers: — You are rather undermanned, and yet this course will serve, that you have taken.

Now Thorvard and his son ride to Espihol, and men were not up when they got there. He met Thorarin and asks: — What action do you intend to take, will you offer Glúm some settlement in the case over the killing?

Thorarin answers: — We think it will be difficult to offer Glúm a settlement.

Thorvard says: — Has there been a summoning in the case or not?

Thorarin answers: — I have not heard about it, but what do you know of it?

He says: — Mar rode this morning with seventeen men to get the case under way, and Glúm stayed at home with five men. Occasion would now be very good to put things right, and this is how you come off poorly, that you do not act swiftly, as Glúm does.

Thorarin answers: — I have no mind to make a trifling counter-charge ready.

Thorvard says: — There is this to consider, were there grounds or not before Steinolf was killed? Did he not seduce Arngrim's wife? Such a charge is surely not worth nothing.

Thorarin answers: — I think ill of moving in such a case.

He says: — What kind of talk is that? Did anything hinder Glúm when he declared Sigmund, your sister's husband, without sanctity before the law? And now there is certainly nothing else for you — you must avoid being so disgraced.

Thorarin says: — I do not know but you may be right.

Then men got up and Thorvald hook pressed for riding to Uppsalir and declaring Steinolf without sanctity before the law.

Thorarin says: — That is not wise, but it is what we shall do.

They came to be fifteen altogether. Seven are named: Thorarin and Thorvald hook, Ketil his son, Arngrim and Eystein the berserk and Thord Hrafnsson who lived at Log Barn and was married to Vigdis Thorir's daughter whom Sigmund had been married to before, and Eyvind the Norwegian; he was at home with Thord.

Now they rode to Uppsalir. Thorvard rode to Ongulsstadir where a good man, Halli the stout, farmed, and sent his son to Thvera and bade him tell Glúm what the Espihol men planned to do: — and then ride back to me quickly.

When Thorvard got to Ongulsstadir, Halli asked what news he had to tell.

None yet, said he. Then he told Halli where things had got to.

And Halli thought he could see how likely it was that he had set all this in motion; said that such men were the cause of great calamity, that he wanted all men to be at odds with one another: — and it would be only right if you were to be killed.

Halli set out quickly with all of his people that he could muster, men and women, and meant to come between the men if need be.

Gudbrand got to Thvera and said that his father had sent him there to tell Glúm the news: — and he said he felt duty bound to let you know what matters to you, that the Espihol men mean to declare Steinolf without sanctity before the law.

Glúm says: – Why did your father not come himself?

He answers: – I call it all one whichever of us has come.

Glúm says: – Your father did well sending you here in case we need men.

He lifted the boy down and tethered the horse.

Then Gudbrand spoke: – My father said that I should come home quickly.

Glúm answers: – No such thing; your father would rather you show your manhood today.

Now Thorvard takes to words: – He is late, my son Gudbrand.

Halli says: – Where did he go?

Thorvard answers: – I sent him to Thvera.

Halli says: – It is well for you to come up against some wily ones; this is as it should be.

The Espihol men rode across the river. Glúm observed their ride and saw that they meant to cross by the Kvarn River ford.

Glúm said that Mar was rather on the late side. Then Glúm ran out after them from the garth, and those with him were six men including Gudbrand. Glúm had his shield and a halberd, and sword girded on; he runs on to the track in front of them and his men after him.

When Thorarin saw him coming he orders his men to ride their straight way and neither faster nor slower: – and no ill can be spoken of us for that.

Thord Hrafnsson asked Thorarin whether they should let themselves be chased, all twenty of them, by Glúm: – though he has five with him.

Thorarin answers: – We shall ride on, for Glúm wants to delay us, and so await his men.

Thord says: — It is no wonder that we often draw the short lot against Glúm when numbers are equal, seeing that you do not dare wait for him now, when he has few men. But he will not chase me.

And he dismounted.

Eystein berserk says he will not ride away: — and let them say they have chased us.

Thorarin says: — That seems unwise to me.

And when Glúm saw that they did not ride on he went slower and shouted his words at Thorarin, and asked what their errand might be to Uppsalir.

Thorarin says they have summoned Steinolf as without sanctity before the law.

Then Glúm spoke: — Is that not much too high-handed, should there not be an offer of terms for it, and might we have some talk towards settling the case?

Thorarin saw that Glúm wanted to delay them and bade his men ride on, and they did so.

Glúm said: — Hold up a while!

But they rode away, and the slower they went the slower Glúm went, and waited for his men, and he spoke: — The case will not be well spoken of if you bring false charges, and there will be disgrace in it then.

We shall not go by that now; you are getting hard to deal with.

Glúm caught up with them and talks to them as they ride and slowed them down so. And when he saw that nothing would delay them and he expected his men, he threw his spear at Arngrim and it went through both saddlebows and his thigh, and Arngrim was in poor shape for fighting that day. Then Eystein was first man to run at Glúm, but Thorvald tasaldi faced him and they two fought, and men thought themselves best off who were farthest from this encounter, for they were both of them fierce and very strong; they struck mighty blows without respite at each other. Thorvald hook made a sharp attack on Glúm with many men and Glúm and his following drew back and defended themselves. But Thorarin did not dismount, for it seemed to him that the odds were enough against one.

CHAPTER 23: A man came running up while they were fighting; he was wearing a leather cloak and had a sword in his hand. He came as Thorvald tasaldi fell before Eystein, and straightway he runs at Eystein and strikes him his death blow. Then he joined Glúm's men and Glúm said this: — You come in good time, Thunderbenda; a good buy it was when I bought you. You will repay your price well this day.

Glúm had a slave who was so named and that was why he said what he did, but in truth this was Vigfus his son, and few or none recognized him except Glúm, because he had been an outlaw for three years and in hiding, and most believed that he had sailed east.

It so chanced when Glúm drew back that he fell and lay there, and his slaves both lay on top of him and were stabbed to death there with spears. Then Mar came up at this moment with his men. Thorarin dismounted and he and Mar fought and no one else took part in it with them. Glúm sprang up and fought as fiercely as ever and now there was no inequality of numbers.

Eirik was a farm-hand with Thorarin. He had been about his work in the morning; he had neither shield nor weapon. He gets himself a cudgel in hand and went in support of Thorarin, and Glúm and his men took the worst kind of drubbing from him, for both men and shields broke before the cudgel he had for striking with.

This is told, that Halldora Glúm's wife called women to come with her: – and we shall bind the wounds of men who are likely to live, from whichever side they may be.

And when she got there Thorarin had just fallen before Mar, and his shoulder was cut open so that the lungs fell out into the wound. Halldora bound up his wound and stayed with him till the battle was done.

Halli the stout came quickly as mediator and many folk with him. The battle ended with five fallen of the Espihol men, Thorvald hook, Arngrim, Eystein, Eirik and Eyvind the Norwegian. Of Glúm's men the fallen were Thorvald tasaldi, Eyjolf Thorleifsson, Jodurr and the two slaves.

Thorarin was brought home with his companions. Glúm too went home with his men and had the dead carried into an outhouse, and Thorvald tasaldi was made ready for burial most worthily; cloths were put under him and he was sewn into a hide.

When folk had got home, Glúm spoke to Halldora: – Our attack would have turned out well today if you had stayed put, and Thorarin had not come away with his life.

She says that there was little hope of life for Thorarin: – but you will have a short while of safety in the district if he lives, and if he dies you will never be safe in the whole land.

Glúm spoke to Gudbrand: – You won much fame for yourself today when you laid Thorvald hook to earth; you gave us good support today.

He answers that it had not been so, though it was true that he had defended himself.

Glúm says: – I saw clearly what happened, a child in age and killed such a champion as Thorvald was, and you will be famous for this deed. I gained honour the same, when I was abroad and slew the berserk.

He answers: – I did not kill Thorvald.

Glúm says: – There is no denying this, friend; you gave him his death wound. Do not turn away from your luck.

He argued so hard with Gudbrand that he believed and acknowledged it, and thought there was honour in it. Nor could he deny it so that it was not held to be true; and then the killing was published as his, and those who had chosen Thorvald to bring a case for thought there was less advantage in it than they had intended.

Men say that Glúm spoke this: – I think it poor that Mar gets himself bandaged because he was given a crack on the head.

He called it that because it was a cross-shaped wound.

Mar answers: – I should have needed it less if I had laid myself down and had my slaves for a shield.

Then Glúm spoke: – Hard mown was Hrisateig meadow today, lads, said he.

Mar says: – For you it will seem hard mown indeed, for you have mown Thveraland out of your hands.

Glúm answers: – I think you do not know that so clearly.

Mar says: – Perhaps I do not know, but for you it will go as though I do.

And when Helga, Glúm's sister, heard the news, she went to Thvera and asked how her son had done his part.

Glúm answers: – There was not found a more valiant man.

Then she spoke: — I should like to see his body, if there is nothing else for it.

This was granted her, and she had him lifted into a cart and gently handled. And when she got him home she cleaned his wounds and then bound them, and so restored him that he spoke.

It was law that where equal numbers fell it should be called an even killing, though there might seem to be a difference in standing; but if one side had suffered more, they should choose the man for whose death a case should be brought. And though something came to light later in the case that would make a different choice seem better, nevertheless the first choice might not be changed. And when Thorarin heard that Thorvald tasaldi was living he chose Thorvald hook, his brother, to bring the case for. But he soon heard that this killing was laid to Gudbrand, and then he would rather have chosen another; nevertheless, the first choice had to stand. They go to see Einar Eyjolfsson. Thorarin says that he would now go back to the contract that they had made between them earlier.

He says: — I have the same feelings about it as when Bard was killed.

Einar took over the conduct of the case at the Thing in summer, and prosecuted Glúm.

Thorarin was laid up with his wounds the whole summer, and so was Thorvald tasaldi, and they both were healed.

Glúm had many supporters at the Thing, and both sides did. A settlement was now sought by high-ranking kinsmen on both sides, and this was agreed as the settlement, that Steinolf's killing should be compensated by lifting the outlawry from Vigfus Glúmsson. Gudbrand was outlawed for the killing of Thorvald, and Glúm got him abroad east. This settled they rode home. Thorvard and Thorarin were ill satisfied with it, and it seemed to Thorarin that he had got no fitting compensation for the killing of Thorvald his brother.

Glúm now lived in high esteem. During the following winter a verse became known that Glúm had newly made: –

> Asks the ale-horn goddess
> own news of my doings:
> talk no more of murder,
> men; matters long ended.
> Let them lie so, woman,
> low. Does this crow-feeder
> call up a last killing?
> Count what that amounts to?

CHAPTER 24: One day when men were at the Hrafnagil hot springs Thorvard came there. He was a great joker and found amusement in many things.

He spoke: – Who is here that can amuse us with new stories?

They say: – There is always sport and pastime where you are.

He says: – There seems no better pastime to me than reciting Glúm's verses, and this is my notion of what he considers short-counted in one of his verses, that he must have short-counted his killings. What must we think? Which must it be? Or which is more likely, that Gudbrand would have killed Thorvald, or Glúm?

For many the second seemed more likely.

He rode then to meet Thorarin and spoke: – I have

done some thinking, and it seems to me that the truth has not come to light about the killing of Thorvald hook, because it can be heard in Glúm's verse-making that he thinks something short-counted of his killings.

Thorarin answers: − I can hardly take up the case another time, true though this may be. It will have to lie quiet now.

That is not wise, and yet it might have lain quiet if it had not been dug up, but now I shall make it known and you will bear such disgrace on account of it that no-one will have borne more.

Thorarin answers: − I think it will not be easy to bring the case before the Althing against the backing of all Glúm's kin.

Thorvard says: − As to that, I can put forward a plan: summon him to the Hegraness Thing; you have the backing of kinsmen there, and there it will be difficult for him to make a defence.

Thorarin answers: − That plan will have to be followed.

With this they part.

Spring turns out poorly, and everything becomes hard to get. It was then that Thorarin made ready the case against Glúm, to be prosecuted at the Hegraness Thing, because all the chieftains belonging to it who should conduct it were bound by ties of kinship with Thorarin. Horses, could hardly cross the moor, however, for the snow.

Glúm took this course: he put a big cargo ship under command of his brother Thorstein, and he was to sail west about, and come to the thing with armour and supplies. But when they were off Ulfsdalir the ship was wrecked and scattered and all were lost together, men and cargo. Glúm went on foot to the Thing with a hundred and twenty men but could come no nearer to tent than in the cordon for three-year outlaws.†

Einar Eyjolfsson had come there with the Espihol men. Glúm was sent word that he should come forward and present his defence. He walks up, but no more room was allowed him than for one. Men were drawn up in two lines, and Glúm was to walk through this pen if he meant to approach the court.

That seemed inadvisable to him, and he spoke to his men: — It is easy to see that they think they have our situation in their hands, and it may be so. I do not want you to turn back now, however. I shall go first, and then two side by side close behind me, and four behind them side by side, and we shall come at a run and hold our spears before us, and the wedge will break through if it is pressed hard.‡

They did so, and ran in one career into the court ring, and it was far on in the night before they were thrust away out, and there was such hard and stubborn thronging that it was late before the judges were seated in court a second time.

As they began to sum up the case, Glúm walks up on to the Thing slope and names witnesses that the sun was now shining on the Thing plain. Then he put them under a lawful ban for the judging of cases and thereupon every case was dropped at the point it had come to.

Men ride away, and the Espihol men took it mighty

---

† cf. p. 131 on Vigfus being made partial outlaw.
‡ Sigmund employs a similar tactic: cf. *Thrand of Gotu*, Porcupine's Quill, 1994, p. 50.

ill; Thorarin calls it shame that Glúm has brought on them.

Einar says: — It does not seem such a loss to me as it does to you, for the case is still there to be taken up where it was left off.

Later the Espihol men ride to the Althing with Einar and many of their friends who had promised to support them against Glúm.

Glúm's kinsmen back him in his suit for a lawful decision; and this is granted on the counsel of wise men provided that Glúm, in answer to the charge, will swear an oath that he did not kill Thorvald hook. Since many had joined in urging it they settled on this, that Glúm should swear the oath that he had not killed Thorvald hook; and it was decided when the oath should be sworn: it was to be in the fall, five weeks before winter. The matter is now so strongly pressed on both sides that the accusation must either go forward in court or he is to swear the oath in three temples in Eyjafirth, and be guilty of oath lapse if this does not take place.

There was much conjecture about it, what kind of oaths Glúm's would be, or how the proceedings would go.

CHAPTER 25: Men ride home from the Thing, and Glúm is at home during the summer. All is quiet in the district. Time comes for the leet and men ride to it, and from it Glúm vanishes, so that nothing was heard of him. Mar stayed at home on the farm.

In the fall, five weeks before winter, Mar called folk in and a wedding feast was arranged, and no fewer than a hundred and twenty men came to it. Everyone thought there was something odd about this feast, for they were of little standing who took part in it. That evening men were seen riding from all the dales in Eyjafirth, two together, or five, and they were gathered into a company as they came down into the district. It was Glúm had come there and Asgrim and Gizur with three hundred and sixty men, and they got to the farm during the night and took part in the feast.

Next morning Glúm sent for Thorarin and bade him come to Djupadal not later than mid-morning to hear the oaths. Thorarin responded and gathered a hundred and twenty men. When they got to the temple six men went in: with Glúm were Gizur and Asgrim, and with Thorarin, Einar and Hlenni the old. The man who was to swear a temple oath took a silver ring in his hand which had been reddened in the blood of a sacrificed ox, and it was to weigh no less than three ounces.

Then Glúm pronounced these words: – I name Asgrim in witness, second Gizur in witness, of this, that I swear this temple oath on the ring, and I say to the god that it was not so: that there I was not, that there I struck not and that there I reddened not point and edge when Thorvald hook met his death. Consider the oath now, men who are wise and are standing here.

Thorarin and his two were not ready to find fault, but averred that they had not before heard it said in those words. In the same way the oath was sworn at Gnupafell and so at Thvera.

Gizur and Asgrim were several nights at Thvera and at their parting Glúm gave the blue cloak to Gizur, and to Asgrim he gave the gold-inlaid spear, and they parted on friendly terms.

During the winter Thorvard and Thorarin met and Thorvard asked: – Did Glúm swear the oath well?

Thorarin answers: – We found no fault in it.

Thorvard says: – It is a thing to wonder at in wise men, that they can be so blind to the truth. I have known such a thing as men acknowledging killings, but I have not known or heard of men swearing on oath that they have killed men, as Glúm has done, for how could he put it more plainly than say that it was not so that there he was not and that there he struck not and reddened not point and edge when Thorvald hook fell at Hrisateig, though he did not say it in any usual way, and this ignominy will never be lived down.

Thorarin answers: – I did not see it that way, moreover I grow weary of having to do with Glúm.

He says: – If you think yourself weary because of ill health, then let Einar take up the case again. He is wise and of good blood, many will back him, nor will Gudmund his brother sit idly by, for what he wants most eagerly is to get his hands on Thvera.

After this Einar and Thorarin meet and put their plan together, and Thorarin spoke: – If you will be in charge of the case many will support you. We shall also do this towards it, we shall buy the land for you at no higher price than Glúm paid Thorkel the tall for it.

Einar answers: – Glúm has now given away the cloak and spear that his mother's father, Vigfus gave him, gifts that he bade him keep if he would maintain his standing, and foretold that without them it would fall away. Now I shall take up the case and press it.

CHAPTER 26: Einar readies the case anew for the Althing, and they crowd there from both parties. And before Glúm rode from home he dreamed that many men had come to Thvera to meet Frey, and dreamed he saw them on the gravel banks by the river, and Frey enthroned. He dreamed that he asked who they might be that had come.

They say: – These are kinsmen of yours who have died, and we make our prayer to Frey that you may not be driven from Thveraland, and to no avail; Frey answers short and angry and remembers the ox that was Thorkel the tall's gift.

Glúm awoke and said he thought worse of Frey at all times afterwards.

Men ride to the Thing, and the outcome of the case was that Glúm acknowledged the killing. And at this his friends and kinsmen put in their word that there should be a settlement rather than a sentence of outlawry or banishment abroad. And they made this settlement at the Thing that Glúm should pay over half of Thveraland to Ketil son of Thorvald hook in compensation for his father, and sell the other half for a price, but he should live on there for that year and then be made outlaw from the district and not live nearer than in Horgardal. They departed after that from the Thing.

Then Einar bought the land, as had been promised him.

Einar's men came there in the spring to work the land and Einar told them that they should report to him every word that Glúm spoke. One day Glúm came to talk with them, and he says: – It is easy to see that Einar has got himself good workmen, and the land is being well worked. Now it is important that both small and great be attended to: you must set up a clothes-drying pole here by the river and it will be handy for the washing of heavy clothing, for the home wells are not good.

Now they come home and Einar asks what they and Glúm spoke about. They tell him how thoughtful he was about everything that should be done.

He says: — Did it seem to you that he would put things in good order for me?

They answer: — So it seemed to us.

Einar says: — It looks otherwise to me. I think that he would hang you on that pole, and he would mean it to be a mockery against me. In any case you shall not go back now.

Einar moved his household there in the spring, and Glúm sat there till the last moving day. And when his men were ready to move away Glúm sat in the high seat and did nothing about going, though he was called. He has had the hall hung with tapestries and will not be dislodged from his land like a low cottager.

Hallbera daughter of Thorodd Hjalmsson was the mother of Gudmund and Einar. She then lived at Hanakamb. She came to Thvera and greeted Glúm and spoke: — Good health to you Glúm, it is not for you to sit here longer. I have brought fire to Thveraland and now I put you out with all yours, and the land is now sanctified to Einar my son.

Glúm stood up then and told her to gabble on like the miserablest sort of old crone she was. Nevertheless Glúm rode away then, and his glance strayed over his shoulder towards the farm, and he spoke a verse: —

> As earls of old, doughty,
> — all men talk about it —
> worked I with my warriors
> a wide swath, sword's pathway.
> So have I severed me

sheer from my dear acres;
ah, one-eyed god's valkyr's
armed one, my good farmlands.

Glúm lived at Modruvellir in Horgardal with
Thorgrim snowstorm and bore with that for no longer
than one winter. Then he dwelt two winters in
Myrkardal. A landslide broke loose near the farm, so
that it took away some houses. Glúm spoke a verse: —

Reave from this ring-giver
rudely his good living
did one blow: bled fortune
buckles; I grow luckless.
Forty years full-hearted
fared I here, unchary;
now, crow-feeder, crowding
come gaunt times upon me.

Glúm bought land at Thverbrekka in Oxnadal and
dwelt there as long as he lived, and grew old and blind.

CHAPTER 27: There was a man Narfi who lived on
Hris Island. He had married Ulfeid daughter of Ingjald
son of Helgi the lean. Their sons were Eyjolf and
Klaeng, Thorbrand and Thorvald. They were all most
able men, kinsmen of Glúm. Klaeng and Eyjolf lived on
after their father on Hris Island.

The man lived at Hagi whose name was Thorvald,
called the manly, and he was married to the daughter of
Thord Hrafnsson from Log Barn, who was called Helga.

One spring Thorvald of Hagi came to Hris Island in a
cargo ship, and meant to catch fish; and when Klaeng

became aware of this he took part in the expedition with him. When both ships came out of the firth they found a whale newly dead, fastened ropes to it and sailed back into the firth with it during the day. Klaeng would tow it to Hris Island because that was nearer than Hagi, but Thorvald would tow it to Hagi and said that was as lawful.

Klaeng says it is not law not to take it nearest where the salvagers own land.

Thorvald claims the right to decide and said that Glúm's kin need not elbow in on their rights: — and whatever the laws may be, the stronger will now have their way.

Thorvald had more men this time and they took the drift whale from Klaeng by force. Both of them were landowners. Klaeng sailed home and was ill content. Thorvald and his men laughed at Klaeng and his men, and said they dared not hold on to it.

One morning Klaeng rose early and rowed with three men in to Hagi; got there early when men were asleep.

Then Klaeng spoke: — We must think of a plan. There are cattle here by the garth and we shall drive them up on to the building over where Thorvald is sleeping and so lure him out.

They did so. Thorvald wakes up and runs out. Klaeng runs at him and gave him a death blow; moved off then quickly and did not dare publish the killing on the spot because many men were at hand; went home out to the island and published the killing there.

Now it was for Thorarin and Thord to ready the case. They called it murder, a killing not properly published. And when this case was brought to the Thing Glúm stayed at home, and during the Thing he rode out to Fljot and Svarfadardal and raised support to confront the court of execution, though he asked that his intention be kept secret.

Klaufi of Bard said: – We shall surely give Glúm support. He was married to Halldora, daughter of Arnor redcheek. Others promised Glúm their support.

Now Glúm rode home.

The case went to a conviction at the Thing. After the Thing Thorarin and Thord readied themselves for the court of execution and had four ships and thirty men on each. Einar and Thorarin captained the ships and came from within the firth towards the island at first light and saw a haze over the buildings, and Einar asked whether it looked to them as it did to him that the haze was not very dark.

They said it looked so to them.

Einar said: – It looks to me as if a crowd is in the building, and that haze will be rising from men. And in case it is, we must make trial and row away from the island openly; then we shall surely know if many men are on the island.

They did so. When the men on the island saw this they ran out to their ships and took after them. It was Glúm had come there with two hundred and forty men, and they chased them all the way in to Oddaeyr, and there was no court of execution. The Eyjafirthers were held in scorn for this.

Glúm stays over the summer on his farm. It was for him to hallow the fall Thing. The meeting place is on the east side of the firth a short way from Kaupang. The Eyjafirthers thronged there in numbers, but Glúm had thirty men only. Many put it to Glúm that he should not go with few.

He says: — I have now lived my fairest years, and I am content that they have not so pressed me that I did not keep to my straight course.

Glúm sailed his ship in along the firth and went ashore and towards the booths. Steep and loose-pebbled gravel banks are there, between the water and the booths. When Glúm came opposite the booths that belonged to Einar, men ran out and bore their shields at Glúm and his few and shoved them down the gravel banks. Glúm fell and rolled with his shield to the flat below and was not hurt, and three spears had stuck in his shield. Thorvald tasaldi had come to shore and saw that it was looking unhopeful for Glúm; he jumped ashore having an oar in his hand and ran up the bank and hurled the oar at Gudmund the mighty. It struck his shield and broke it in pieces, and a piece of the oar hit him in the chest and he fell senseless and was borne in a cloth by its four corners to his booth.

Then each side egged the other on to attack, and they hurled missiles at each other and fought with stones, and it developed into a hard fight, many were wounded, and all said the same thing, that never might few men more valiantly defend themselves than Glúm and his men did. Einar and his men attacked hard. Then men came between them and the outcome was that two men fell of Glúm's company, Klaeng Narfason and Grim bankleg, brother of Halldora, Glúm's wife. Then Brusi Hallason spoke this verse: —

> Gave what I got, even;
> gainsaid their vain boasting.
> Truly, men are telling
> tales now, how I flailed them.

Goddess of gold, headlong
their going was, heels showing,
wind-swift, that I wondered
where to they were faring.

Einar spoke a verse: −

Budged that edge-brandisher
backwards from attackers;
thronged at the Thing, sliding,
thought I was hard fought with.
Sadly that sea-stallion
skipper, failed to grip his
heels to hold in gravel
hard, at the sea's margin.

Then Glúm spoke a verse back at them:−

Unwilled went helmeted
warriors over shore-cliff;
risk raised not their spirits,
rueful their deeds proved them:
fierce-handed they found us
flashing shields, unyielding.
Gorged blood-greedy ravens,
gourmands on that sand-spit.

The cases were settled thus: the deaths of Klaeng and
Thorvald of Hagi were paired, and the killing of Grim
bankleg was equated to the injury to Gudmund. Glúm
was ill-satisfied with this settlement, as he made clear in
this verse, which he composed afterwards: −

Ills old earth are spoiling;
age the poet plaguing;
battle storm abating
that bore my years forward.
My good hand is hindered,
held back from just action;
bold Bankleg killed, meanly
bides, vengeance denied him.

CHAPTER 28: It was one summer as the brothers
Gudmund and Einar were riding from the Thing that
Glúm called men to him, and sent the men up to
Oxnadal moor to invite the brothers to his home and
say that he would settle all differences between them: —
for I am now good for nothing on account of age, and it
is not just to meat that I am asking them.

Glúm was then blind. He had a watch kept on their
coming. Gudmund would accept the invitation but Einar
would not, and each rode his own side of the river.

Glúm was told that one group was riding towards
him.

Then Einar is unwilling to accept my invitation; he is
so full of doubts that he trusts no-one.

The story tells that Einar called across to Gudmund
and said: — I shall come there in the morning if you go
there this evening.

Gudmund pondered what he said: — Your meaning
must be that you will have to prosecute on my account.

He turns to follow Einar.

Glúm is told that neither has turned his way.

That is an ill turn, then, said Glúm, for if I had gone
to meet them I was bound I should not miss both.

He had a long knife bared under his cloak.

And that was the end of dealings between Glúm and the Eyjafirthers.

When Christianity came here to Iceland Glúm was baptized and lived three years after that. He was confirmed in his last illness by Bishop Kol and died in white raiment. At that time Mar Glúmsson dwelt at Fornhagi, and he had had a church built there, and Glúm was buried there and Mar as well, when he died, and many other people, because for a long while there was no church in Horgardal except only that one.

What men say is that for twenty years Glúm was the mightiest chieftain in Eyjafirth, and for another twenty no-one was better than equal to him. What they also say is that Glúm was the doughtiest of all fighting men here in the land. And with this the saga of Glúm ends.

End-notes

CHAPTER 1: **To go east from Iceland** always means to go to Norway.

CHAPTER 4: **Pair-drinking**: the text says *tólfmenningr*, 'twelve-man drinking' here, but I have followed Turville-Petre's advice in his note and called the custom 'pair-drinking'. He suggests that the Icelandic represents a scribal error. The word *tólfmenningr* does not occur elsewhere in Icelandic, nor is the custom known. In pair-drinking, *tvímenningr*, couples chosen by lot would each share the same drinking horn. There was also a drinking custom known as *sveitardrykkja* in which one horn would be passed around the whole company.

CHAPTER 5: **Temple** *(hof)*: no convincing evidence has been found that would suggest what form the temples of pre-Christian Iceland might have taken. There may have been no separate buildings or shelters; places of worship may have made part of the main longhouse of a farmstead. Sacrifices were most likely to have been held in the open air, though certain cult feasts would need ample indoor accommodation. Thirty-seven Icelandic farms are known that have, or had, the name *Hof* or *Hofstaðir*, a number which comes close to that of the thirty-nine priest-chieftaincies that existed after c. 965.

CHAPTER 4 & 6: **Berserk**: there are accounts in Old Icelandic literature of berserks who could rouse themselves to fight with more than human frenzy, and in this mood be proof against pain. Some kings were said to be glad to have berserks among their fighting men. Some of the family sagas tell of berserks who go about as roving bullies, challenging men to fight with them, for a woman, for property or for the mere sake of fighting, as do the two in Viga-Glúm's saga. The name is sometimes interpreted to mean bear-sark, though in Old Icelandic the form *ber* for bear appears infrequently, and then as a suffix. A tapestry found in the Oseberg Ship pictures a male figure who seems to be clad in a bear skin. There is no certainty, however, that berserks did wear bear skins, nor that they were shape-changers, and they seem, for the most part, to have been in control of their beast ferocity.

CHAPTER 6: *Dísir*: in poetic compounds, *dís* was a general word for goddess. It is the second element of many feminine names such as *Thordís, Vigdís* and *Halldís*. The plural, *dísir*, usually refers to female guardian and fertility spirits, to whom seasonal sacrifices were made. They were not distinct persons, as the gods and goddesses were.

CHAPTER 7 & 8: **Vitazgjafi**: the field is named only in these two chapters of the saga. In Chapter 8 Glúm makes the pregnant observation to Vigdis when he meets her and Sigmund on the field that *'Eigi brásk hann Vitazgjafi enn'* – 'Vitazgjafi again has not failed us'.

Its exact location is not known, though the saga tells us that Glúm rode 'southwards over the river' to come to it. It was therefore near Frey's temple, which was also 'south of the river at Hripkels-stadir'. It was a choice field in that 'it was never barren' and this suggests that it was a Frey's field, sacred to Frey, the god of fertility. Any violent act committed on it would be a sacrilege. Glúm, however, is confident of the luck and personal authority that has been passed on to him by his maternal grandfather, and is willing to risk the god's displeasure (cf. General Introduction, pp. 15–16).

Vitazgjafi, the choicest bit of Thveraland, was allotted to both Hallfrid and Astrid (and Glúm) when the property was divided after Eyjolf's death; they were to have it in alternate years, a not uncommon way of allotting such a treasure at the time. The name takes a form of a kenning (cf. the appendix on the verses). The first element, *Vitaz*, is the genitive singular of a past participle, *vitaðr*, from the verb, *vita* (know), and means 'appointed', 'fixed' (cf. Turville-Petre's edition, p. 61). The second element is an agent noun formed from the verb *gefa* (give). The literal translation of the entire name is 'giver of what is assured': a field in whose crop one may have confidence. As the name of the field where Sigmund was killed, Vitazgjafi first appeared in Viga-Glúm's saga. There is a reference to the killing in the early versions of *Landnámabók*. The eldest of these says that Glúm killed Sigmund *á Sigmundarakri*. 'in Sigmund's grainfield', i.e. in the grainfield that gets its name from Sigmund, who was killed there. The other versions simply say that he killed him *á akrinum*, 'in the grainfield', which later redactors then identified as Vitazgjafi, doubtless from their knowledge of the saga. 'Sigmund's grainfield' thus appears to have been the name for the field that was current in the twelfth century, and presumably some thought they knew where it was.

The field cannot have been known when the saga was composed, for the writer, who was clearly well acquainted with the locality of the story, refers to it in the past tense. It seems likely that the name only exists by virtue of its appearance in the saga and there, perhaps, only because Glúm used it in a memorable phrase that stayed with Vigdis from the morning when her husband was killed.

CHAPTER 9: The noun '**fetch**' translates the Icelandic word *hamingja*, which is derived from *hamr* meaning 'skin' or 'shape'. A man's *hamingja* was his guardian spirit, which stayed with him during his life time and transferred itself to a younger kinsman when he died. Another word with a similar meaning was *fylgja*, which was derived from the verb that means 'to follow'. *Hamingja* seems to have meant something more personal than *fylgja*, though the two words were used virtually as synonyms. The word 'fetch', given as substantive 2 in the OED, 'The apparition, double, or wraith of a living person', is suggested by Turville-Petre in his note to this passage. It seems to be the only English approximation to *hamingja* or *fylgja*, and I have preferred it to some sort of explanatory substitute.

When Glúm summons Sigmund, having dug up his body as one without sanctity before the law, he is in effect declaring that he has no legal rights. Other instances of the digging up of a body for legal purposes occur in *Njála*, chapters 55 and 64. After the conversion to Christianity such disturbance of the peace of the grave was forbidden (cf. Jónas Kristjánsson, IF IX, p. 33, n.1)

CHAPTER 17: **Fostering** was generally considered to be the task of an inferior. Sometimes, however, between men of comparatively equal rank, one would offer to foster another's child as a conciliatory gesture, to settle a difference, or as a form of compensation. Hallvard was a slave who had been freed by Glúm. The author calls him Vigfus's foster-father, and Vigfus shows a loyalty to him that is not uncommon, in saga literature, between men and their foster-parents. Perhaps Hallvard, while he was still in Glúm's household, had been 'tutor' to Vigfus; the author may have used the title rather loosely. Fostering ties often seem to have been as strong as those of kinship.

A twelve-man verdict might be called for as a means of proof in cases involving theft, as in this chapter, or perhaps sorcery, perjury or other offences against the public interest. It was one of a chieftain's duties to appoint such a jury and act with it. In case of a disagreement on a verdict, 'then those in the majority are to prevail, and if they are in equal numbers they are to give the verdict the chieftain wishes' (cf. Dennis, Foote and Perkins, p. 76).

CHAPTER 19: **Vigfus made partial outlaw**: cf. the general note on Law and Government (p. 131).

CHAPTER 25: The equivocation in Glúm's oath hangs on a point in Icelandic grammar that seemed impossible to put into English. The substitute English equivocation was provided by Peter Foote. I must also thank him for the concluding couplet of the stanza on p. 146, in which Glúm betrays himself.

CHAPTER 24: Courts might sit through the night. This would not be in darkness at the Althing, since when it met there were twenty-four hours of full or all but full daylight, and even during the other assemblies the hours of darkness would be short. Verdicts were to be given before the morning sun shone on the field of the Thing. Turville-Petre notes that Glúm's employment of this veto is unusual but valid (cf. Dennis, Foote and Perkins, p. 75).

Glúm's Kin on His Mother's Side

Eymund field-spoiler
|
Viking-Kari

Bodvar

Astrid   Olof = Teit
| |
Eirik   Gizur the white
|
Astrid   Thorstein   Vigfus = Hallfrid
| (Thorkel's daughter)
Olaf Tryggvason

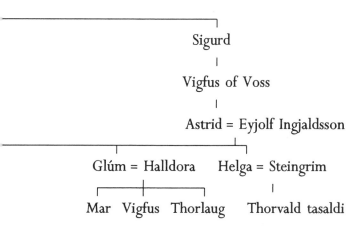

Sigurd
|
Vigfus of Voss
|
Astrid = Eyjolf Ingjaldsson

Glúm = Halldora   Helga = Steingrim

Mar Vigfus Thorlaug   Thorvald tasaldi

Glúm's Kin on His Father's Side

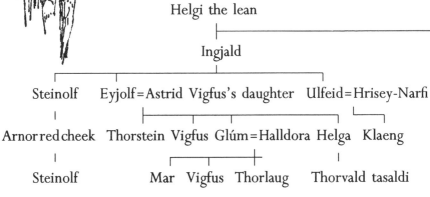

Helgi the lean

Ingjald

Steinolf   Eyjolf = Astrid Vigfus's daughter   Ulfeid = Hrisey-Narfi

Arnor redcheek   Thorstein Vigfus Glúm = Halldora Helga   Klaeng

Steinolf   Mar Vigfus Thorlaug   Thorvald tasaldi

1. (as above) Hamund darkskin = Helga Helgi's daughter

Yngvild sister of all

Thorvard of Kristness

Gudbrand

Ingunn = Hamund darkskin[1] = Helga = Audun the rotten[2]

Thorir of Espihol = Thordis Kadal's daughter

Thorarin   Thorvald hook   Thorgrim   Ingunn   Vigdis

Arngrim

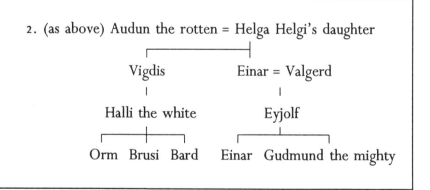

2. (as above) Audun the rotten = Helga Helgi's daughter

Vigdis   Einar = Valgerd

Halli the white   Eyjolf

Orm   Brusi   Bard   Einar   Gudmund the mighty

A Note on the Verses: Both Sagas

Two different stanza forms are represented in the verses
in 'The Saga of the Schemers': 1, 2, 4, & 6 are composed
in the commonest Eddaic measure, which is known as
fornyrðislag, 'ancient lay'; 5 and 6 are in the most highly
developed of the scaldic metres, the *dróttkvætt*, 'noble
metre'. *Fornyrðislag* is a comparatively uncomplicated
verse form, common to the West Germanic languages as
well as the Norse. Its rhythms are flexible and especially
suited to longer narrative poems but they may also be
terse, as they are in both Ofeig's and Ospak's verses.
There are no examples of *fornyrðislag* in 'Viga-Glúm'. In
'Schemers' the translation of the four *fornyrðislag* stanzas
reproduce the sense of the originals closely and they keep
to the stanza form as well. This calls for lines of four
syllables, paired by alliteration. Two syllables in each line
are more strongly stressed than the other two. For
example, the stanza on p. 51:

> No honour now
> to name my son;
> not a mention
> make of him here:

In the first two lines, two of the stressed syllables –
now and name – carry the alliteration. The other two
stressed syllables are hon and son. The first syllable,
'No', is not part of the scheme of alliteration since it is
not stressed. In the Icelandic the lines are:

> *Fýrr var sœmra*
> *til sónar húgsa;*

gét ek <u>á</u>ldregi
<u>Ó</u>dds at sínni;

The stresses are marked with acute accents and the alliterating letters are underlined. It should be noted that any vowel may be in alliteration with any other. A literal translation of these lines would be:

Formerly there was more honour in thinking of my son; never do I speak of Odd, at the moment.

The rhythms of all four of these *fornyrðislag* stanzas are strong, and their syntactical structure is closely knit, almost like that of the *dróttkvætt* except that it is straightforward. Ospak's stanza, the only poem included in the K version of the saga, has a poetic weight comparable to that of the *dróttkvætt*, whereas Ofeig's stanzas are ironic and lighter in mood. In longer narratives the *fornyrðislag*, in its tightlipped way, may become very powerful.

For an example of the *dróttkvætt* I shall take Glúm's first stanza, Chapter 7:

<u>Bear</u> in on the <u>bor</u>ders,
<u>bold</u> ones, of my <u>hold</u>ings:
green walls I begrudge their
greed. Let them heed, woman.
<u>In</u>jure my <u>an</u>cestral
<u>a</u>cres, who mis<u>take</u> me:
sword leaps from my scabbard
swift, as my heart lifts it.

The syntax divides into two statements, each of four

lines, and inter-related as to sense. The alliteration in the first two lines falls on b: Bear, borders and bold, and these are, appropriately, the first and third stressed syllables of the first line and the first stressed syllable of the second line. The same pattern obtains in the fifth and sixth lines, and it should be noted here that in accordance with alliterative practice, any vowel may alliterate with any other: Injure, ancestral and acres. There are six syllables per line, three of them stressed, and the final syllable is always unstressed. The first and penultimate syllables of all lines should be stressed; in the odd lines these syllables should also be half-rhymed; in the even lines they should be full-rhymed. In the first line of the quoted *dróttkvætt* these are Bear and bor- and in the fifth, In- and an-. Similarly, in the even lines the corresponding syllables have full rhyme: bold and hold- and ac- and -take. It should be said that the same pattern applies to lines 3 & 4 and 7 & 8.

Scaldic poets developed a poetic diction based initially on the kenning, a symbolic or representational device common to the known Germanic poetry, familiar to students of Old English poetry in such figures as 'whale's road' and 'gannet's bath' for the sea, or 'speech bearers' for human kind, 'battle flame' for sword, and many others. The scalds developed this device to such a degree that they would have kennings within kennings. In this translation kennings of the simplest degree only have been attempted, and they will offer no better than a glimpse of scaldic diction. The scalds also used archaic words that had an allusive value, derived from old stories. Men and women were seldom referred to directly in their poetry, nor were gold, battle, ship and many other simple nouns. Yet many of the poems were forceful and expressive of strong and deep feelings.

No attempt has been made to English the kennings or the single allusive nouns in Ofeig's first *dróttkvætt* stanza (Ch. 8, p. 53). In his second *dróttkvætt* (Ch. 10, p. 68) 'dwarf's mead' is a kenning for poetry, drawn from a story recorded in the section on poetic diction, *Skáldskaparmál*, of Snorri's *Edda*. The story tells of two dwarves, *Fjalar* and *Galar*, who kill the wise man *Kvasir*, creature of the gods — the *Æsir* and the *Vanir* — and make mead from a mixture of his blood and honey. Whoever drinks this mead acquires the gift of poetry — *skáldskapr*. The second kenning is *hatlands*, an obvious substitute for 'heads'.

Viga-Glúm was a scald, hence the verses in the text of his saga, at any rate in their earliest manuscript forms, were probably his. They high-light points in the narrative and contribute to its tone of historical truth, besides introducing passages of dense verbal texture amid the spareness of the prose. Glúm's second, fifth and sixth verses are prophetic dream poems that concern events in the story. His seventh verse proves fateful. It is a boastful verse, as many scaldic verses were. Other such verses in the saga are the first, fourth, eighth and twelfth, and also Brusi Hallason's and Einar Eyjolfsson's verses, numbers ten and eleven. Glúm's ninth and twelfth verses sound a regretful, elegiac note.

The verses in 'Viga-Glúm' are all composed in the *dróttkvætt* form, including the lines in Chapter 16, the Cavern episode, except that in these four the internal rhyme scheme is defective. The morphology of Old Icelandic allowed the scalds to make use of elaborate inversions and interpolations in their sentences. These were important to their style, but they are out of reach for modern English, which has virtually no inflections and must therefore keep to a fairly straightforward sentence structure if it is to make sense.

The rhyme, alliteration, stress pattern and syllable-count are not hard to imitate, allowing for an occasional deviation. The poetic diction, however, is difficult, because many of its elements are unfamiliar. I have no more than suggested a few of the kennings and allowed some inversion, interpolation and ellipsis in the English to give a hint of the involute scaldic word order.

VERSES IN VIGA-GLÚM:

PAGE 97: There are no kennings in the translation. The woman addressed in the fourth line is Astrid.

PAGE 104: The head-dress goddess, whom Glúm saw faring hugely forth firthward, is Vigfus's fetch. 'Head-dress goddess' is a simpler kenning for woman than it is in the Icelandic, which might be translated literally as 'goddess of the fire of the hawk's island'. 'Goddess' is a frequent base word in kennings for women, paired with attributes associated with women such as 'gold', 'adornment', 'threads', 'head-dress' and others. The original kenning may be analyzed as follows: the 'hawk's island' is the arm, which is the resting place of the hawk in falconry, and the 'fire' of the arm is gold. Fire is so frequently a base word for gold that in many scaldic kennings it is virtually a synonym for it. 'Fire of the arm' refers to the significant functions of the arm, or hand, in wearing or distributing gold. The original kenning is therefore 'goddess of gold'.

There are three more kennings in this stanza: 'warfare's dreadful deity' and 'slain men's greeter' represent valkyrs, the choosers of the slain in battle,

who are to be carried to Odin, and both stand for
Vigfus's fetch. They are grammatically in apposition, in
the nominative. 'Tree of battle' is a common kenning
for man or warrior, and here it is in the vocative. The
second quatrain of the poem is therefore addressed to a
man, though no man is identified in the text.

PAGE 135: 'Warrior' in the second line represents Mar,
to whom the poem is addressed. There are several
kennings in the Icelandic, but they have not been
attempted in the English.

PAGE 136: The kenning of the first two lines represents
Thorarin, subject of the first quatrain. Here, as
elsewhere, I have followed Turville-Petre's
interpretation of the Icelandic, which is 'God of the
battle of Limafjord bear cubs', in which 'Limafjord bear
cubs' is a kenning for ships. Limafjord stands for 'fjord'
in general. I have taken only the ships part of the
kenning and substituted 'storm-elks' for 'Limafjord bear
cubs' in order to make the alliteration.

PAGE 146: The 'ale-horn goddess', subject of the first
clause, is a woman, presumably Glúm's wife, Halldora.
The literal translation of this first kenning would be
'protecting goddess of the wine cup', but demands of
translating this meaning into *dróttkvætt* in English were
responsible for the other. The text in *Möðruvallabók* has
only six lines, and there must have been a concluding
couplet which suggested that the count of Glúm's
killings was one short. The couplet included in this
translation, needed for the story's sake, was composed
by Peter Foote, and I thank him for it. The stanza is
meant to be a riddle, and a risky one at that.

PAGE 153: The 'one-eyed god's valkyr's armed one'
addressed in the last two lines of this verse is a man, but

there is no indication in the text of who he might be. A literal translation of the kenning from the Icelandic would be 'bender of the ski of Odin's goddess', Odin's goddess being a valkyr, her ski a sword and the sword's bender, or wielder, a warrior.

Kennings in the last five stanzas are fairly obvious. A 'ring-giver' (page 154) is a man, here Glúm himself. A 'goddess of gold' (page 158) is a kenning for woman; it is in the vocative case, but there is no woman to whom it might be addressed. An 'edge-brandisher' and 'sea-stallion skipper' (page 158) are kennings for man, and both refer to Glúm. These are the translator's kennings, rather freely adapted from originals in the Icelandic, the second quatrain of which Turville-Petre says 'presents difficulty'. In this poem Einar is both exulting and ironic: 'Nothing,' he says, 'hindered Glúm's flight; he found no grip for his heels in the sandbank.'

A Note on Law and Government

The first landtakers in Iceland were Norwegians, some
of them men of rank, with their followers, families and
slaves. Most came from Norway itself, but some were
re-settlers from Ireland, Scotland and the Scottish Isles.
Other free and aristocratic farmers followed from
Norway, established themselves on the land and attached
themselves to the chieftains for mutual support. Such
attachment was not necessarily on grounds of proximity,
but it was most likely to be so. No agreement bound
the settlers to consult or act together until early in the
tenth century, sixty years after the first landtakers
arrived. The land was then considered to be fully
occupied, and the need for such an agreement, and some
kind of country-wide legal and administrative structure,
became apparent. The settlers, aristocrats and others,
had already been used to some self-government in
Norway in the form of assemblies called 'things', in
which they had discussed and ordered matters of
common concern. The chieftains who came from
Norway had left that country, at least partly, to distance
themselves from the thrust towards kingly centralized
authority that Harald finehair was making, and in remote
Iceland they found a land of their own that required no
such central authority, with its retainers and bodyguard
and its costly army and navy. They soon felt the need,
however, for a code of laws first, and then some
regularity of meeting for settling differences, interpreting
the laws and passing judgements. They sent a man named
Ulfljot to West Norway to study the newly established
code there, the Gulathing Law. After a three-year stay
he came back and presented the code he had drawn up

and in 930 it was accepted. It called for an annual
assembly from the whole country at which chieftains and
their followings met for a fortnight in the summer, and
this became known as the Althing.

Chieftains of the first assemblies were those referred to
in the first chapter of 'Viga-Glúm' as having the ancient
chieftaincies; there seem to have been thirty-six of them.
The Icelandic title for chieftain, was *godi* which is to say,
'having to do with gods', and from the beginning a
primary function of Icelandic chieftains was to serve as
priests in the temples they had had built on their lands for
the worship of the old gods, most probably Thor or Frey.
The name given to a chieftain's authority was *godord*. The
functions the two words *godi* and *godord* represented seem
to be peculiar to Iceland, though the word *godi* occurs
contemporaneously on the Glavendrup Stone on the
island of Fyn. The duty and privilege of hallowing the
country-wide Althing was reserved to chieftains in the
line of Thorstein, son of Ingolf, the first settler of Iceland.
Local things, sometimes called *leidar* (sg. *leid*) – translated
as leets – were hallowed by local chieftains. With the
conversion to Christianity in the year one thousand, the
chieftains' priestly function lapsed, though in the
somewhat unformed state of Icelandic Christianity during
its early years some of the chieftains preserved a next to
priestly authority in the new churches they had built on
their lands.

Not all of the mightier landtakers became chieftains,
and although a certain prestige was attached to the title,
as appears in Odd's acquiring of his, it seems to have
been principally a public service willingly taken on. It
was not necessarily inherited, though it normally seems
to have been, and it might be bought, sold, bartered and

even shared among two or more holders. It might also be taken away for certain lapses in the carrying out of its duties.

The legal and administrative responsibilities of the chieftains were mostly fulfilled at the Althing. This was held at an admirable site chosen by Ulfljot in the southwest of Iceland, at a location central to the most populous parts of the country, though so far from settlements in the northwest and east that the journey from them by horse would take days, or perhaps weeks. While they were attending the Althing chieftains and their men sheltered themselves in booths on the grounds. These were tents of homespun (*vadmál*) erected each year over more or less permanent walls of stone or turf. A mixed crowd of tradesmen, smiths and vagrants also attended, staying in a variety of booths and temporary shelters.

There were two types of court at the Althing, legislative and judicial. The legislative court had chieftains for its members, each attended by two advisers; it interpreted the laws, made new laws and granted exemptions from them. The other type of court had free men, who were not chieftains, for its members; it heard cases and pronounced judgements. The enforcing of the judgements was left to the injured parties, if need be with the help of a local chieftain.

The most important single official at the Althing was the Law-speaker. He was elected by the legislative court. He was the only salaried member. His term of office was three years, and during it he recited from memory the whole body of the laws, one third each year, with assistance, if his memory needed it, from five or more men conversant with the law. He might be reappointed any number of times. Besides reciting the laws he decided when the judicial courts should convene and led them out to their separate places on the grounds, and in general he took charge of all affairs of the Althing except the hallowing. He was nearest to being a central authority in Iceland but he had no powers, only the respect that was given him by virtue of his office. The memories of the successive lawspeakers and other men 'conversant with the laws' were their repository until they were codified in 1117-18.

Four judicial courts were established, one representing each of the four quarters into which the country had been divided for administrative purposes. The division took place in or about 965, when three more chieftaincies were added in the north quarter, and the total number of chieftaincies was raised to forty-eight.†
A fifth court was established, primarily as a court of appeal; cases that the quarter courts had dismissed because of failure to agree on a verdict were tried in the fifth court. It was also a court of the first instance for certain charges, such as those involving the giving of false testimony, offering of bribes in quarter courts, or sheltering of outlaws, debtors in bondage or runaway slaves. Members of these courts were appointed anew each year by the chieftains, and they might be challenged and replaced. Procedure was a matter of great importance in the conduct of cases, and a charge might be invalidated by a mere failure to observe correct procedure, as all but happened to Odd's charge against

---

† See the separate note on Odd's purchase of a new chieftaincy, p. 73-74.

Ospak. There were thirty-six judges in each court, appointed by holders of the 'full and ancient chieftaincies', and each court seated itself in a circle on the ground.

Local things or assemblies were also established, to be held in the spring, and sources seem to assume that they would normally meet. Three places were fixed for them in each of the east, west and south quarters, and four in the north. Important local cases might be tried at them, though these would more likely be taken straight to the quarter courts at the Althing. Local things had no legislative function, but there were decisions they might make within the law, affecting their own districts. Judicial cases of minor importance were regularly tried in their courts, debts were paid at them and local prices were set by them. Late summer local meetings, the 'leets', which were also known as things, met usually on the same sites as the spring Things, at more or less regular times. They were brief, not more than two days and a night, and their primary function was to report on what had been decided at the Althing. All these local meetings were hallowed by holders of the 'full and ancient chieftaincies', and Glúm's assertion of his right to hallow the fall meeting near Kaupang is evidence that he was a chieftain, though the text of his saga nowhere specifically states that he was. His attempt led to the battle in which his brother-in-law Grim bankleg and the outlawed Klaeng lost their lives.

Many lesser offences, and some serious ones, were settled out of court by payments of money. Such a settlement provides the principal action of 'The Saga of the Schemers'. In private settlements atonement payments might be assessed on self-judgement by the injured party, or decided by an agreed third party. Private settlements might also require the man with the weaker case to move from his locality, the kind of internal banishment suffered by Glúm. Cases that were brought to court were given verdicts of 'guilty' or 'not guilty'; the law was then consulted for specific penalties. These were most often fixed fines and compensations for damage. Serious offences would be penalized by outlawry, which was of two degrees. Lesser outlawry meant banishment for three years from Iceland, allowing the outlaw, *fjörbaugsmaðr*, to leave the country unmolested within three years.† This was Vigfus's first penalty. Full outlawry meant deprivation of all rights and, in effect, death. Vigfus became full outlaw when he failed to abide by his sentence of banishment. Glúm, however, kept him hidden till the sentence of outlawry was lifted in the settlement that followed the battle of Hrisateig.

The law demanded that a wrong be formally published, either by the wronged one or by someone acting for him. A personal injury must also be declared by the one who has inflicted it, near where it had been inflicted, and in a clearly audible voice. *Morð*, a killing that had not been formally published, was the most serious crime of all, and for it there could be no defence. Klaeng was summoned for *morð* because he had failed to publish the killing of Thorvard where it had taken place. In the same way, Ospak was guilty of *morð* for not having published the killing of Vali.

Summoning of the guilty might be in the spring, as

---

† The Icelandic for a fully outlawed man was *(sekr) skógarmaðr*.

near the guilty one's home as it could be safely carried
out, or otherwise the prosecution might simply be
presented at the Althing. Odd rides out to summon
Ospak for the stealing of his sheep. Vali intervenes and
is murdered by Ospak, and instead of summoning Ospak
for this Odd elects to proceed against him with a panel
of neighbours whom he calls to attend the Althing as
backers of his case. He then commits a procedural error.
When one of his panel dies he forthwith fills his place
from among the neighbouring farmers. He should have
waited till he got to the Althing and made up the
number there.

Prosecution for any injury was prepared and
presented by the wronged one, or by a more powerful
member of the family, the more powerful, popular and
legally skilled the better. A woman's case would always
be presented for her. Thus Astrid asks her son Thorstein
to present the defence on her behalf for her slaves.
Witnesses played an important part in all cases at law,
though they would more likely testify to procedural
correctness than to the circumstances of the crime, or
whatever matter was in hand.

Sentences were left to be carried out by the injured
party, with the help of his chieftain if he needed it, in a
court of execution. A strong body of men would be
important in most such actions. The court of execution
that was to carry out the sentence on Klaeng was
frustrated by the force that Glúm raised to oppose it.
Klaeng's outlawry was not lifted by this, and he was still
under sentence of death if the men of Espihol were to
find occasion to carry it out, but then he was killed in
the fighting that Glúm brought on when he attempted to
hallow the fall thing at Kaupang.

WOMEN IN THE SAGAS: The world of the sagas is predominantly masculine, yet in few of them are women so entirely out of the picture as in 'The Saga of the Schemers'. Svala is the only woman with any part to play, and for that she is given no character. Viga-Glúm's story, however, brings in several women, all with distinctive roles and characters. Astrid is the first and most prominent. She fights for her land against Thorkel and Sigmund as well as she can and then clears her frustration in a fairly typical way for saga women; she sends Glúm out to deal with Sigmund in an action that perhaps won him his by-name 'Viga', killer. Halldora, Glúm's wife, plays a sympathetic part, nursing Thorarin at the Hrisateig battle and so saving his life, and she has a pregnant reply for Glúm's criticism. Similarly, Glúm's sister Helga literally brings her son, Thorvald tasaldi, back to life after the same battle. Hallbera's dismissal of Glúm from Thveraland at the last is full of wit and experience. And there are minor women whose brief appearances are noteworthy and poignant: Vigdis, who sees Glúm kill her husband and is brusquely sent home with the news, Arngrim's sharp-tongued wife and Una, who foresees her husband's death, and falls in a faint. The author of Glúm was aware of feminine attitudes in what was very much a man's world.

Index

Names referring to people are in roman type; all others are in italic.
The names, Iceland and Icelandic, which occur *passim* are not included.
[S] and [V] refer respectively to 'The Saga of the Schemers' and 'Viga-Glúm's Saga'.

Ivar [V] 84–88, 90, 91

Jarnskeggi Einarsson [S] 47, 49, 57, 59, 63, 68
Jodurr [V] 137, 143
Jorunnarstadir [V] 124

Kadal [V] 92, 108
Kalf (Barn-Kalf) [V] 115–17
Kaupang [V] 156
Ketil Thorvaldsson [V] 139, 152
Ketilbjorn from Mosfell [V] 105
Klaeng Narfason [V] 154, 155, 157, 158
Klaufi Thorvaldsson [V] 107, 156
Kol, Bishop [V] 160
Kollafirth [S] 31
Kristnes [V]137
Kvarn River ford [V] 140

Langadal [S] 38
Laugardal [S] 49, [V] 129
Laugaland [V] 137
Law Rock [S] 46, 61
Leet [S] 34, 36
Log Barn farm and *Log Barn* [V] 115, 117, 139, 154
Lon [V] 107
Lump, see Eyjolf Ingjaldsson

Mar Glúmsson [V] 113, 114, 116, 124, 135–38, 140, 142, 144, 149, 160
Mar Hildisson [S] 71–72
Mel, Melsland [S] 31, 32, 35, 36, 40, 48, 53, 54, 58, 59, 69, 72
Midardal [V] 120, 128